'The thing to remem————————
vampires,' said Elsa, 'is t————————
ruthless. Nothing and ————————
in their way. So I've got one very important
piece of advice for you. If you should locate
the vampire leader, whatever you do, don't
look directly into his eyes.'

'In case he hypnotizes us, you mean?'

'He may do that,' said Elsa, 'but much
more likely . . .' She hesitated for a moment.
'Well, if you let him, a vampire will try and
get right inside your head and pick things up
from you, such as your secret nightmares.
And then he will use this information – to
torment you.'

And suddenly I was filled with terror . . .

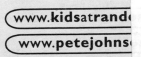

How many Pete Johnson books have you read?

Vampire Titles

THE VAMPIRE BLOG

'You can't knock a Pete Johnson book . . . a goodly dollop of fangly terror. Perfect'
The Bookbag

Thrillers

AVENGER

Winner of the 2006 Sheffield Children's Book Award
'Brilliant' *Sunday Express*

THE CREEPER

'Explores the subtle power of the imagination' *Books for Keeps*

EYES OF THE ALIEN

'Very readable with a skilful plot' *Observer*

THE FRIGHTENERS

'Prepare to be thoroughly spooked' *Daily Mail*

THE GHOST DOG

Winner of the 1997 Young Telegraph / Fully Booked Award
'Incredibly enjoyable' *Books for Keeps*

TRAITOR

'Fast-paced and energetic' *The Bookseller*

PHANTOM FEAR

Includes:
MY FRIEND'S A WEREWOLF *and* THE PHANTOM THIEF

Funny Stories

THE BAD SPY'S GUIDE

Shortlisted for the 2007 Blue Peter Book Award
'This book grabs you from the first page (5 stars)' *Sunday Express*

HELP! I'M A CLASSROOM GAMBLER

Winner of the 2007 Leicester Our Best Book Award
'A real romp of a read that will leave readers ravenous for more' *Achuka*

HOW TO GET FAMOUS

Winner of the Sheffield Community Libraries Prize

HOW TO TRAIN YOUR PARENTS

'Makes you laugh out loud' *Sunday Times*

RESCUING DAD

'Most buoyant, funny and optimistic' *Carousel*

THE TV TIME TRAVELLERS

'Another great humorous book from critically acclaimed Pete Johnson' *Literacy Times*

TRUST ME, I'M A TROUBLEMAKER

Winner of the 2006 Calderdale Children's Book of the Year

THE VAMPIRE HUNTERS

Pete Johnson

CORGI YEARLING BOOKS

THE VAMPIRE HUNTERS
A CORGI YEARLING BOOK 978 0 440 86939 9

Published in Great Britain by Corgi Yearling,
an imprint of Random House Children's Books
A Random House Group Company

This edition published 2011
3 5 7 9 10 8 6 4

The Random House Group Limited supports The Forest Stewardship
Council (FSC®), the leading international forest certification
organisation. Our books carrying the FSC label are printed on FSC®
certified paper. FSC is the only forest certification scheme endorsed
by the leading environmental organisations, including Greenpeace.
Our paper procurement policy can be found at
www.randomhouse.co.uk/environment

MIX
Paper from
responsible sources
FSC® C016897

Set in Century Schoolbook

Corgi Yearling Books are published by Random House Children's Books,
61–63 Uxbridge Road, London W5 5SA

www.**randomhouse**.co.uk
www.**totallyrandomhouse**.co.uk
www.**kids**at**randomhouse**.co.uk

Addresses for companies within The Random House Group Limited
can be found at: www.randomhouse.co.uk/offices.htm

THE RANDOM HOUSE GROUP Limited Reg. No. 954009

A CIP catalogue record for this book is available from the British Library.

Printed and bound by CPI Group (UK) Ltd, Croydon, CR0 4YY

This book is dedicated to all the many readers who wanted me to write a sequel — and had strong views about what should happen next. I hope I've got it right!

A note from the Author:

This story is fiction – but although vampires are creatures of our imagination, there are other dangers to be aware of. Both Tallulah and Marcus know that Tallulah is taking a big risk in going to meet someone whom she only met through the internet. This can be very dangerous and is something you should never do in real life.

For information on how to use the internet safely, check out:

www.thinkuknow.co.uk
or
http://kids.direct.gov.uk

Hi.

I'm Marcus, and if you're reading this now, then I'm in massive trouble.

This is a top-secret blog, which if it got into the wrong hands could cause terrible damage. And by the wrong hands, I mean every single human being. Yes, even you.

No human can ever be trusted with my sensational news.

Yet up to the night of my thirteenth birthday I was as normal as you – or so I thought. Then my parents told me they were half-vampires and I was about to start changing into one too. I thought they'd gone insane until I found a white fang dangling just inside my mouth.

Since then I've had a blood craving at school, got poisoned by a pizza (it had garlic in it) and been attacked by a vampire. Oh yeah, they exist too. Only it's animal blood they like, not human. There's just one exception – the blood of half-vampires before they change over.

That's why a vampire called Karl tracked me, and even conned his way into my house, claiming to be a long-lost relative. Karl tried to get me to drink this drugged potion he'd prepared. Then he attacked me, and if it hadn't been for . . . Tallulah.

Yeah, it was a girl who saved my life. Just two weeks ago: a girl who's mad about vampires too. But afterwards my parents had to hypnotize poor Tallulah into forgetting everything she'd seen. I hated that moment. But like I said, no human must ever discover our true nature. That's the first and most important rule of being a half-vampire.

Well, can you imagine the carry-on if humans ever discovered there were half-vampires living down their road? We could tell them we're completely peaceful but they wouldn't believe us. And we'd be forced to live in a zoo – or maybe somewhere even worse.

But very unfortunately the hypnotism

didn't completely work. Tallulah still remembers little fragments of what happened — but only in dreams. These dreams fascinate her, though. And she believes they mean something.

Then last week two people were attacked in nearby Brent Woods. There have been all sorts of stories of wild, savage creatures jumping out of the air at their victims. And the local paper is full of theories. Some kind of wolf? A vicious fox? A wild animal which has escaped from the circus . . . ?

But Tallulah's convinced it's a vampire. Now, I know for certain vampires have no interest in humans or their blood. I can't tell Tallulah that as she'd wonder how I could be so sure. But I keep throwing scorn on her vampire theory.

To be honest, I'm totally sick of vampires and half-vampires, and now I've changed over I just want to concentrate on the human part of my life. But Tallulah's up to something. I know she is.

And this worries me.

This worries me a lot.

CHAPTER ONE

The Vampira Website

A message you must read from Vampira:
Do you think vampires only exist in stories? If you do, leave this page now and don't bother coming back either. We have nothing in common and you're just wasting my time.

But if you believe vampires might be real, then read on, as I have great news for you.

I've always sensed they existed, but now I have definite proof. Recently I've been dreaming about vampires every single night. Only I know they're more than dreams — they're like secret messages which I'm somehow picking up when I'm asleep. I've obviously got tons of undiscovered special powers, which doesn't surprise me at all. I've long suspected it, actually.

I've been trying to work out what these dreams mean. And now I know. You've probably read about those two attacks in Brent

Woods. Well, I can tell you, they're not by wolves or foxes — they're by vampires. And my dreams have actually been warning me about them for days.

So if you've got any information about vampire activity, contact me now, if not sooner. I'm especially interested in vampire sightings around Great Walden, near Basing, because that's where I exist.

Rest assured, everything you tell me will be highly confidential and I am totally serious.

So come on, let's shake things up a bit and find the vampires, which I know are much closer to us than people think.

Kitty: posted 2 days ago
Hi, Vampira, I'm sure I've seen a vamp. It was a man, out one night in such a weird costume like he'd popped out of another century. And he had really dark eyes and pale, white skin. He gave me such a shock, I yelled out: 'Hey, vampire!' and he looked very angry, as if he knew I'd discovered his deadly secret. I couldn't stop shaking afterwards.

Vampira answers:
He could have just been coming from a fancy-dress party for which he wore a bit of make-up. And a lot of people would be cross if you called out: 'Hey, vampire!' at them. I believe 100% you haven't seen a *real* vampire.

Libby: posted 1 day ago
Vampira, I want to tell you about this really gorgeous boy with very
pale skin who lives near me. Well, the other night I saw him and
called out his name and when he turned round his eyes were bright
red. He's got to be a vampire as he's scary and yet so cute, just like
the boy from 'Twilight'.

Vampira answers:
He could have been wearing red contact lenses or maybe you just
imagined it. I'm 200% certain he's not a vampire. And this is *not* a
dating website.

Goth-girl: posted 6 hours ago
Hey, Vampira — I LOVE, LOVE, LOVE vampires and I can't stop think-
ing about them. I want to be one with all my heart. I've even got a
T-shirt that says: BITE ME AND WE'LL BE TOGETHER FOR ETERNITY.
Do you keep hoping a vampire will bite you at night? I bet you do.
Let's meet up soon. I live in Winchester, so not too far away.

Vampira answers:
Your T-shirt is revolting and so are you. And I never, ever want to
meet up with you. I don't want any more time-wasters on my site
either. Only people like me who know vampires are here *now*.

CHAPTER TWO

Monday 5 November

1.05 a.m.

Here are the advantages of being a half-vampire:

I DON'T HAVE TO GO BED UNTIL HALF-PAST ONE IN THE MORNING.

I CAN FLY – OR FLIT, AS WE CALL IT.

And that's it. I can't think of anything else.

And those advantages aren't as hot as they look because there's not a whole lot to do in my house late at night (or any other time, actually) and usually I just end up hanging out with my parents for hundreds of extra hours. Personally I'd rather be asleep.

And as for flitting – well, I've gone right off that too.

Here's why.

To go flitting all you have to do is walk about on tiptoe – just as if you're about to do a spot of ballet dancing for a few seconds, while at the same time emptying your mind so you're thinking of absolutely nothing.

Then after a bit your feet aren't on the ground any more. You're whooshed up into the air and, before you know it, transformed into a bat as well.

Fantastic.

Well, it was the first time I tried it. And I stayed up in the air for five spine-tingling minutes. Only last night I couldn't get off the ground. Just spent ages tiptoeing around with absolutely nothing happening.

So tonight my parents decided we'd have a flying lesson in the back garden. Now, our garden is well hidden from prying eyes with massive fences, but even so my parents reckoned they couldn't do anything until all the lights in nearby windows were extinguished. So I was hanging about waiting for ages until, at half-past twelve, the three of us trooped outside.

Dad whispered to me, 'Now, first of all it's important you're relaxed.'

But nothing makes you tenser than someone telling you to relax, does it? And straight away I felt myself stiffen.

Dad went on, 'You're probably a bit worried you let us down last night when you didn't get airborne.'

'Excuse me, but how is you saying all this supposed to relax me?'

'What I wanted to say is, you haven't let anyone down. And last night was just a blip, all right?'

'Thanks for clearing that up, Dad.'

'I want you to breathe not through your mouth but through your nose. Do you think you can manage that?'

'I'll do my best,' I said. And I took two deep sniffs through my nose.

'There,' said Dad, 'I bet you're feeling relaxed already, aren't you?'

'Actually, I'll feel a lot more relaxed when you stop talking, Dad,' I said.

'Fair enough,' said Dad.

He went and stood by Mum, who was

swinging a stopwatch about: 'So, in your own time now, Marcus.'

I started hopping about the garden on tiptoe. I looked just like a little kid who's desperate to go to the loo.

'You still seem very tense,' said Mum. 'Really relax those shoulders.'

'And keep on breathing through your nose,' said Dad.

'And remember to think of nothing,' cried Mum.

'And we know you'll crack it tonight,' said Dad. They went on whispering 'encouragement and advice' while fifteen minutes thudded past – and I was getting more and more frustrated while my feet remained obstinately on the ground.

Then Dad said, 'Why not just copy us?' Of course, he and Mum were up in the air and transformed into bats in the blink of an eye. And when you can't do something and somebody else does it – instantly – well, that's just about the most humiliating thing in the whole world, isn't it?

That's why, without another word, I stomped inside and tore up to my bedroom.

1.20 a.m.

Now I feel a bit pathetic about running off to my room. But I'd just flitted so easily before. And even though I don't care at all about being a half-vampire, I'm really annoyed I can't flit any more.

1.27 a.m.

My parents think I'm cool about being a half-vampire now. But that's one thing I am good at – pretending. I only dare tell the truth when I'm on my iPod touch, which is no bigger than a mobile so it travels everywhere with me. At any moment I can turn to my blog – hidden behind a top-secret password, of course – and put down stuff which no one else must ever know.

For instance, I haven't got my head around being a half-vampire at all. And there are times – loads of times, actually – when I just feel like a total freak.

1.45 a.m.

Mum and Dad have just piled into my bedroom. 'We want to give you a chance to calm down. And you're not to worry,' said

Dad, looking very worried.

'And we've brought you something,' said Mum.

'Food?' I asked hopefully.

'No, it's a poster,' said Dad, 'for half-vampires like you, who are experiencing a few little teething problems.'

'We hope you like it,' said Mum.

I opened it up. It was a picture of a sky plastered with annoyingly glittery stars, and in big letters were the words: YOU HAVE A GIFT, and underneath it in bright blue: SO AIM FOR THE STARS. And flying into those words were two bats. I could only stare at it for several seconds. Its total ghastliness temporarily robbed me of speech.

'Would you like me to put it up in your bedroom?' asked Mum.

'If you do, I'll sleep in the garden,' I said.

Mum sighed deeply and said, 'Well, just study it now and soak up its glorious message.'

'If I look at it any longer, Mum,' I said, 'I'll need sunglasses. Those stars aren't just bright . . .'

Mum snatched the poster away from me, sighing heavily.

The Vampira Website

Bela-Hale: posted 2 hours ago
Hi, Vampira, I don't believe in vampires. And I think you're a bit mad.
No offence. Also, you're a big show-off, telling everyone about your
dreams and how you think there are vampires attacking people in
that wood near you. But what are you doing about it? Absolutely
nothing.
　　Sorry, but that's what I think.

Vampira answers:
You are entitled to your opinion, however stupid. And I am going to
do something about the vampire attacks. In fact, I shall be going
to Brent Woods to keep watch very soon. I just want to get some
more info first. But I know I am right. Vampires are close by.

Mrs Elsa Lenchester: posted 5 minutes ago
Dear Vampira,

By a very lucky twist of fate I discovered your page and was fascinated by it. I do not believe you are a show-off at all. And I too believe in vampires.

Even stranger, I also live in Great Walden and I am certain that your dreams are really warning you about these attacks in Brent Woods. But before you do anything else you must talk to me. I have some vital information which I believe will change your whole life. Would you mind coming to me, as I am quite elderly and do not go out very much these days.

Vampira answers:
What you said interested me greatly. Let's meet up really soon.

CHAPTER THREE

Monday 5 November

8.15 a.m.

I'd just finished breakfast when Dad handed me a little bottle of blood. 'Now, we'd like you to take this to school with you. I expect you're wondering why.'

'Is it to pour over my chips?'

Dad shook his head and didn't smile. 'One day – maybe quite soon or maybe not for weeks and weeks – you will have an attack of blood fever. Two attacks, in fact, are usual.'

I stared at him. 'Just hold on a second here. I've changed over into a half-vampire. So this weird stuff is behind me now.'

'I think we did mention to you there's a Phase Two,' said Dad.

'And it's not weird stuff, as you put it,' said Mum, joining us. 'It's a perfectly natural—'

'Perfectly natural,' I interrupted. 'Excuse me, but who else in my class, in my year – in my entire *school* – will be taking a bottle of blood to school with them today?'

'What we mean is,' said Dad, 'and I would ask you to keep your voice down at all times when discussing family business; it's a perfectly natural occurrence for us. Well, your mum and I have been through it, and look at us.'

'Exactly,' I muttered. 'No, it's just after all the earlier carry-on, I really thought I could stay still for a bit now and just be normal.'

'But we're perfectly normal,' said Mum.

I started to laugh until I saw I was the only one. So then I said, more than a bit wearily, 'Come on then, tell me all about blood fever.'

'One day soon,' said Dad, 'a deep craving for blood will strike you. It will overwhelm you, in fact, and be all you can think about.'

I thought back to just before my change –

there had been a day or two when all I'd been able to think about was juicy, bloody steak and the like. Was this going to happen *again*? And *worse*?

'So if this happens to me while I'm at school,' I said, 'I just pull out my trusty bottle, glug down all its contents and then smack my lips and tell everyone: "Aaah, that blood slips down a bit lively. You should all try it."'

A look of total alarm now crossed both my mum and dad's faces.

'I'm joking,' I cried. But neither my mum nor my dad are at all hot on jokes and both now looked very anxious. 'Hey, fear not, I know I've got to sneak off to a secret place—'

'Just ask to be excused,' interrupted Mum gravely, 'and be very sure you are unobserved by anyone before drinking the blood down. And then remember to wipe your mouth very carefully. Afterwards, you may still require more blood. If you do, you are to ring your dad or me immediately and just say these three words: "I'm still thirsty!" Can you remember that?'

'If I try really hard, I might.'

'Then we will rush to wherever you are

with reinforcements,' continued Mum. 'Meanwhile, if anyone asks you what this bottle is, you say it's cough medicine.'

'No one's heard me cough for five years, but I'm sure they'll believe that,' I said.

'Well, you might give the odd cough now and again,' suggested Dad.

'Like this, you mean?' I said, and let out this really deep death-rattle of a cough.

Dad did give a tiny smile then, but Mum said firmly, 'No need for such theatrics, and we have actually slipped a cough-medicine label on the bottle.'

'So you have,' I said.

'Now let us watch you hide the bottle safely away in your trouser pocket,' said Mum. 'And I still haven't sewn up that hole in your left pocket – remind me to do it tonight. So you must put it in your right pocket.'

I did this and then Dad said, 'Of course, this blood fever attack might not happen for weeks or even months yet.'

'But it could happen very soon indeed,' added Mum.

8.35 a.m.

And I've got a sneaking suspicion they'd *like* it to happen very soon. In fact, this whole blood fever thing has got them both buzzing.

But not me.

I *hate* it when things happen to me which I can't control or stop. It makes it seem that I'm turning into someone who's not me, Marcus Howlett. That's why I don't want to waste another second thinking about blood fever.

Instead, I want to totally concentrate on normal stuff like . . . well, on Saturday Joel (my best mate) and I went to this firework party. And we got chatting to these girls – nothing serious, just fooling about. But there was this one girl, Katie, who goes to our school, and Joel reckons he's going to ask her out today. I'll believe that when I see it.

But, just between us, blog, I wouldn't mind a girlfriend. Feel I'm ready for one now. Nothing too serious. But yeah, it'd be cool. Probably.

12.05 p.m.

Joel's still going to ask Katie out – only not in

person. He says if she rejected him, the shame would make his head explode. So he's sending someone else to do this little job for him – me. It's one of the duties of a best mate, apparently.

12.30 p.m.

I saw Katie leaving the dining hall and she was on her own. So here was my chance. Joel was hanging about pretending to text someone and trying to look casual. But really he was watching out for me to tap my ear twice. That was our secret signal, which meant Katie had said 'Yes'. Clever or what!

So I sped over to Katie and started gabbling, 'How are you, Katie? And how would you like to go out with Joel on Friday night? And will you answer the second question first? In fact, you can forget the first one altogether. So how about it?'

Katie gaped at me. She'd also gone very red. So I rushed on, 'No pressure at all, but if you turn Joel down I don't think he'll ever get over it. So if you say yes, you'll be saving a life. How about that? Would you like to save Joel's life?'

Katie was sort of laughing now, but still not saying anything, so I said, 'Joel's taking you to the cinema, by the way, and I should have told you that before. I'll stop here now so you can say yes.' I paused in a highly expectant fashion.

Katie was still laughing in an embarrassed way, but then she said quietly, 'Just ask Joel to come and speak to me when he has a spare moment.'

While not a definite yes, it sounded incredibly promising. So after tapping my ear twice I said, 'Actually, I think Joel is around here somewhere. Why — would you believe it? — there he is.'

The casual note I was trying to add to the proceedings was somewhat spoiled by Joel tearing over to us like a lost puppy.

But as he and Katie grinned at each other, I knew my work there was done. In fact, I don't think either of them even noticed me leave.

12.40 p.m.

Joel's in such a good mood he's started to feel sorry that I haven't got a girl to go to the

22

cinema with on Friday. 'There's got to be a girl somewhere who'll go out with you,' he said, 'and I'm going to track her down. No matter how many centuries it takes.'

12.50 p.m.

Actually, I know who I'd like to go to the cinema with – and this is yet another deep, dark secret – Tallulah.

Joel says Tallulah can cheer up any room the instant she leaves it. She's one of those people who's in a permanently bad mood. She never seems to care how she looks either. But that's part of what I like about her. And I do think she's really striking-looking – and yeah, attractive.

And lately I'd got to know Tallulah quite well. And when she's not at school, I sort of miss her.

12.55 p.m.

You won't believe what Tallulah has just done.

I've just been looking at this new website she's set up for loonies – sorry, vampire fans. She's tried to disguise her identity by calling herself Vampira – but everyone at school knows it's Tallulah and thinks it's so hilarious.

Except me.

The last thing I want is Tallulah telling other people about those dreams. And what if she starts remembering even more? *We can't allow Tallulah to know vampires exist.* Those were my mum's very words before she and Dad hypnotized all Tallulah's memories of that encounter away. They don't know anything about these recent dreams of hers. They'd go mad with worry if they did.

And, of course, I know what vampires are really like. They're vicious, mean creatures – to be avoided at all times. Tallulah hasn't a clue what she's messing with. Not that I was expecting any real vampires to contact her website. No, it would be just weirdos.

But even they could be pretty dangerous.

12.59 p.m.

Tallulah's had the morning off for some reason. But as soon as she turns up at school

I'm going to get her to close down this lunatic website.

1.05 p.m.
Tallulah's just arrived. So here goes.

CHAPTER FOUR

Monday 5 November

1.15 p.m.

Tallulah strode into school, scowling fiercely.

And when she saw me, she started yawning.

'Oh, charming,' I say.

'I'm just so fed up,' she said, 'that everything annoys me.'

'No change there then. So where have you been all morning?'

She shrugged. 'At the doctor's – well, that's what I'm telling them.'

Then I remembered I was angry with her and said, 'Oh yeah, a little question for you. Are you totally insane?'

'Probably. Why do you ask?'

I looked right at her. 'Vampira.'

She started. 'How do you know about that?'

'The whole school knows about it. You do realize you've just opened up your life to every spooky, not-to-be-trusted, deeply dodgy person around.'

'Well, they've got to be an improvement on the stiffs at this school.'

'No, Tallulah, you've got to close down this website.'

'Why?'

'I've just told you why.'

'Don't you start talking to me like a teacher.'

And I was so mad keen to pull her away from this website, that's exactly how I was sounding. So I said, a bit more gently, 'I'm not. I'm talking to you as your friend.'

She actually twisted about a bit uncertainly when I said that.

Then I added wildly, 'I'll do anything to get you to close this website down – anything. I'll even invite you to come to the cinema with me on Friday. See the sacrifices I make to keep you out of trouble.'

I really had meant this to sound funny and light-hearted but it totally, totally backfired and Tallulah snapped, 'Talk about bigheaded. Why on earth should I want to go to the cinema with you?'

'Did I mention I'll throw in a free choc ice and as much popcorn as you want to throw at me?'

'Do me a favour, will you?' she cried.

'Just name it.'

'Don't ever speak to me again.'

Before I could reply she'd stormed off.

1.20 p.m.

I make just one stupid comment and I've destroyed a friendship. I'm . . . But that's all I want to say about it right now.

1.25 p.m.

I've just told Joel. He said, 'Oh, Tallulah will calm down – in a few years.' Then he added, 'And why on earth did you ask her anyway? You're not that desperate.'

No one gets Tallulah – except me. And we really did have a good friendship until I messed everything up. I've got to sort this out.

4.15 p.m.

I thought I'd wait until after school to talk to Tallulah. So I hung about outside the gate. I knew exactly when Tallulah was coming because half the school chanted 'Vampira' after her.

She shook her head angrily at them and didn't look exactly pleased to see me either. 'I've got nothing to say to you,' she snapped, and rushed off.

I raced after her. 'Hey, are you entering the Olympic walking championship or something? Can't you just slow down a bit?'

'No.'

She continued walking at a breakneck speed and I suddenly realized she was going in completely the opposite direction to her house.

'Hey, where are you going?'

'None of your business.' She continued walking even faster, but then suddenly stopped and hissed, 'Once I'd have told you, even asked you along.'

'Well, tell me now. Look, you can be Vampira for the rest of your life if you like. I think you're mad, but it's your life.'

'Oh, thank you,' she said with undisguised sarcasm.

'And I promise I'll never, ever ask you out to the cinema again.'

'Good,' she practically shouted, 'because I'll never go with you either.'

'Well, now we've got that sorted out, where are you going?'

She looked at me for a moment before saying quietly, 'I'm going to see someone who has definite proof that vampires are real.'

I groaned loudly and then asked, 'How do you know she has this proof?'

'She told me.'

'Great, and which one is she? She's not this . . . Mrs Lenchester, the one who said she's going to change your life for ever?' I looked at her. 'It is, isn't it? You're off to see a woman you don't know anything about – and have you told anyone where you're going? You know what we've been told at school about never meeting anyone off the internet like this!'

'It's none of the school's business,' said Tallulah, 'and it's nothing to do with you either.'

'Well, I'm coming with you then.'

'Oh no, you're not.'

'Look on me as your new bodyguard. You get a free trial all afternoon.'

'Don't bother, you're sacked already.'

Then Tallulah raced off at an incredible speed.

Now, I'm a boy of many talents – but running definitely isn't one of them. I don't just come last in cross-country, I arrive back three days after everyone else. So I was soon puffing and panting and really struggling to keep up with Tallulah, especially when she went charging through Brent Woods, leaving me far behind.

Brent Woods is not my favourite place, especially after I got attacked by a vampire there. And now at night there's some wild creature on the rampage. I tell you, even in late afternoon, it's got a spooky atmosphere and it's not exactly safe for anyone on their own. Then right behind me I heard a scuttling, rustling sound. I whirled round. Nothing. But I had a creepy feeling that someone – or something – was watching and following me.

I was so glad to get out of there. Ahead was the common and the cricket pavilion, where Tallulah used to hold her Monsters in School meetings. This was how I first got to know her, when she set up a kind of secret society for people who loved horror stories.

But today she went tearing off in the other direction to the pavilion, while I just had to stop for a minute. And as I struggled to get my breath I thought: What am I doing? Why didn't I just let Tallulah meet this woman? She's almost certainly a loon but probably totally harmless.

But then a mad idea stole into my head. What if Mrs Lenchester was only pretending to be an old lady? After all, we only had her word for it. She might not even be a woman at all. No, she could be some mean guy who wanted to lure Tallulah to his house with all this stuff about changing her life for ever.

Suddenly I was running faster than I've ever done in my whole life. No wonder my head was just spinning. Ahead was the river, over which was a small stone bridge. And I could just make out Tallulah crossing it.

Now we were into the oldest part of the

village. There were some big, expensive houses here. I tore past all these and up this old road. There were bungalows, then all by themselves at the top were two old cottages. Opposite them were just hedges and trees. So it was a great spot for someone who was a bit of a recluse – or a nut-job. I saw Tallulah knock on the door of the end cottage.

She'd gone inside the cottage before I reached it. I lay on the ground for a moment, getting my breath back. (I'm just not designed for strenuous exercise.) No one seemed to be about at all. In fact, this could easily be the quietest road in the world, neglected and forgotten by everyone. Even the birds here were chirping really quietly. They probably know they've got to whisper, as the average age of people who live here is about ninety-six.

I edged a bit closer to the cottage, just to check I couldn't hear any sounds of Tallulah screaming or being generally tortured. Nothing.

In fact, now I was here I was pretty sure Tallulah was safe in that cottage. But I had to be totally certain. And anyway, after all my effort getting here, it seemed a bit tame just to scuttle home now.

I could ring on the doorbell, except there wasn't one – just an old-fashioned door knocker. Should I knock? But how could I explain what I was doing here? Then I had an idea which made me smile a lot.

And I rapped loudly on the door.

CHAPTER FIVE

Monday 5 November

5.25 p.m.

A dim light shone through the door's front glass and then the door creaked open about a millimetre. 'Can I help you?' asked a soft, husky voice.

'Oh, hi, I'm Marcus – Tallulah's boyfriend.' And I had to swallow a laugh as I said this. 'She told me to meet her here.'

The door opened wider, revealing an elderly woman in a brightly patterned flowered dress and squeaky slippers, whose arms were jangling with gold bracelets. She had wispy honey-coloured hair, large dark eyes, and was leaning heavily on a stick.

'I didn't know her young man was coming too,' she said.

'That's Tallulah – always forgetting about me.'

'Well, Marcus, I'm Elsa Lenchester. Very pleased to meet you.'

We shook hands and she glanced at me but then stopped and stared – I mean, really stared as if she was memorizing my face. But then she obviously decided I was all right because she said enthusiastically, 'Ah yes, you must definitely be a part of this. Yes, indeed. Come inside, Marcus.'

I stared at her warily. She went on: 'Call me Elsa, and then I shan't feel as old as I undoubtedly am. Now, we're just in here.'

She led me past a dingy old mirror and down a passage steeped in darkness. Then she opened a door into a surprisingly large but very dark room with a heavy, musty smell of carpets, and old books – the room was crammed with them. On one table was a huge vase of flowers, while beside it stood a tiny crystal ball on a stand. That gave me a handle on Elsa. I bet she was well into magic and performing little tricks. I could imagine her as a magician's assistant or an actress in her youth.

Tallulah was perched on a large green sofa which had undoubtedly seen better days. She gave a splutter of shock when I plonked myself down beside her. And when Elsa said, 'You didn't tell me your boyfriend was coming,' she had a coughing fit. 'Poor boy, must be feeling quite neglected,' said Elsa. 'I'll just get another cup. Are you all right, dear?'

Tallulah nodded, while still coughing violently.

'Don't worry, I'll look after her,' I said, hiding my grin.

Elsa shuffled off while I started patting Tallulah on the back. 'How's that, darling, feeling better now?'

Tallulah gasped. 'I've been called some insulting things, but your girlfriend is undoubtedly the very worst.'

'So a quick kiss is out of the question then?'

'I'm here on a very serious mission and if you spoil this I'll kill you. That's a definite promise.'

Then Elsa returned. She put my cup down on the little table beside us and asked, 'Not bothered about cats, are you?'

Both Tallulah and I shook our heads.

'Good, because this house is full of them.'
And as she said this, a large Siamese cat
slunk in, followed by a huge tortoiseshell
tom. They sat, inspecting us solemnly.

'How many cats have you got?' asked
Tallulah.

'Do you know, I'm not really sure. Cats are
such free spirits. And I let them come and go
as the fancy takes them. But I know I've at
least eight regulars, as I call them.'

'It's like you're running a hotel for cats,'
I said.

Tallulah immediately frowned at me. But
Elsa tilted back her head and laughed.
'That's exactly what I'm doing; only I don't
charge for my accommodation. Still, you
haven't come here to talk about cats . . . it's
vampires you're interested in.' And quite
suddenly the old lady's face darkened. 'I can't
tell you how pleased I am to hear from you
because I've been so worried.'

'About what?' asked Tallulah at once.

'About the vampires, of course. And one
new sect of vampires, in particular, which is

worse than any of the others. We're all in so much danger. And yet no one has ever listened to me – well, until now.'

I looked at her closely. Was she going to turn out to be a demented old bat, after all? Well, that's what I wanted. Then Tallulah would realize the kind of people who were hooking up to her website and just forget the whole mad idea.

Then I noticed Elsa was staring back at me. 'They think I'm just an old fool,' she said, as if reading my thoughts. 'But they're the fools' – her voice rose – 'never once suspecting that another secret world exists alongside ours. How can they be so blind?'

'I know,' cried Tallulah.

She spoke so keenly Elsa smiled and said, 'But tell me first about your dreams, dear.'

Tallulah began. 'For weeks now I've dreamed about vampires every night. The first dream, I found him—'

'Your boyfriend . . .' interrupted Elsa.

Tallulah wrinkled up her nose as if she'd just smelled something disgusting and whispered, 'Yes.'

'You see, Elsa, she just can't stop thinking

about me,' I said, and grinned at Tallulah, desperately trying to lighten the atmosphere.

But Tallulah didn't smile back. Instead, looking right at Elsa, she said, 'He was in the woods. And he had the mark of the vampire on his neck. The next time, there was a mad vampire in his house about to attack him. I saw the vampire's face really clearly. The night after that I saw the vampire . . .' And so Tallulah talked on and on, ending, 'There's not a night now when I don't dream about vampires.'

'And is this young man here always in your dreams too?' asked Elsa.

'Er, yes,' said Tallulah reluctantly, 'I suppose he is.'

Elsa suddenly stumbled to her feet. 'Stand up a minute, my dear,' she said to me.

I hauled myself to my feet and then she seized my hand. And she was looking at me so intently I felt a bit uneasy. So of course, I made a joke. 'Hey, you're not going to ask me to dance, are you?'

She gave a soft chuckle. Her eyes were so dark; you couldn't even make out her pupils very clearly. And all at once they were beamed right on me. Shivers ran through me then. She gripped my hand more and more tightly.

'Oh yes, I can feel it,' she said, and turned to Tallulah. 'Now I know why he's in all your dreams.'

'It's my amazing good looks, isn't it?' I said. 'Many have commented on it.'

'Shut up,' snapped Tallulah.

'She loves me really,' I began.

Then I noticed Elsa seemed to have gone into a kind of trance as she murmured, 'I sensed it the moment he was at the door. I know these things and I'm never wrong: never.'

She was holding my hand so firmly now I murmured, 'You've certainly got a strong grip.'

This seemed to bring her round and she let go of my hand very suddenly. 'I'm sorry, it's just I'm so excited because – you're one, aren't you?'

5.36 p.m.
And that, blog, is when I got really scared.

CHAPTER SIX

Monday 5 November

5.37 p.m.

'Don't be afraid, dear,' Elsa went on, moving away from me. 'It's all right to admit it, you know. I've known for years that people like you existed. And you don't frighten me at all.'

I could only gape at her, too horror-struck to even speak. Was she about to expose me as a half-vampire? Next moment there was a dark flash and something hurled itself at me, hissing and shaking with rage.

It was as if some mad demon had suddenly been set loose. Tallulah sprang up and was about to come to my aid. But instead, Elsa gave this low whistle, more like a wail really.

And immediately the tortoiseshell cat instantly leaped off me again and hung his head. 'Yes, you should hang your head, you vexatious cat. I'm so sorry about that. I hope he didn't hurt you.'

'Oh no, no,' I said, stunned by what had just exploded onto me.

'When I first took Rufus in, he did that all the time,' she said. 'He was a real hell-cat. He was always flying at me, until one day I said to him, "Rufus, I've never given up on a cat before, but I'm giving up on you if your behaviour doesn't improve!" And do you know what, from that instant he totally changed and now he always wants to have his tummy rubbed.'

'I'll take your word for that,' I said.

She picked up the cat, which had now turned into the calmest, gentlest one you could ever meet. 'I can only apologize again,' said Elsa. 'But when Rufus meets strangers, his old nature asserts itself.' Then she gave me one of her piercing stares. 'But we were interrupted. You were about to tell me you are one, weren't you?'

Here was that question again. Was she

about to break my cover? It'd be total shame and humiliation if she did. For the first rule of being a half-vampire is to keep the secret at all times.

Then she went on, 'You're a sensitive, aren't you?' and relief just shot all through me. But Elsa went on watching me. 'You see things. You know things, and at times your power terrifies you, doesn't it, Marcus?'

'Well, it just doesn't seem fair,' I said, 'with all my charm and good looks and brilliant sense of humour, to have special powers too. I mean, come on, give someone else a chance.'

Elsa smiled faintly, but went on studying me, which was more than a bit unnerving, actually.

Then came a loud, indignant cough. 'What about me?' demanded Tallulah.

Mrs Lenchester turned to her. 'You have great enthusiasm – and that's very important too.'

For a moment Tallulah looked devastated. After all the attention Elsa was lavishing on me, just being told you have enthusiasm was like being handed a real booby prize. But then Tallulah said loudly, 'But I'm the one

44

who's been having the dreams. I'm the reason we're here now.'

'Well, you could have a gift I haven't spotted yet,' said Elsa, 'but I picked up his special powers right away.'

I gave Tallulah an I-can't-help-being-brilliant smile, which made her frown really heavily before saying impatiently, 'Will you tell us about the vampires now, Elsa?'

Elsa nodded, closed her eyes and then murmured, 'My late husband Fergus and I were on the stage.' But I'd guessed that already. 'We never hit the heights, but we travelled the world.' She pointed to some framed photographs behind her. 'However, my late husband's real interest was in magic and the supernatural. We visited so many strange and magical places, and wherever we went we picked up stories of vampires. The real ones, who live on the fringes of every society, hidden away from humans—'

'But secretly feeding off their blood,' interrupted Tallulah.

Elsa shook her head wearily: 'No, no, a silly myth. Vampires actually take blood from animals, not humans. They dislike the taste of human blood; to them it has a very sour flavour.'

Tallulah jumped in surprise. And I tried to look amazed too. But this was very similar to what my parents and Dr Jasper – the half-vampire doctor they had brought in to check me over once – had told me about vampires. I looked at Elsa with a new respect.

'So vampires,' she continued, 'have practically ignored human beings for centuries. But now there are pockets of vampires who say humans *should* be attacked – not for the taste of their blood, but for another reason entirely. They believe human blood – if drunk often enough – can give vampires new strength and power, while draining humans of their *energy* of course. They are the most dangerous vampires in the whole world.'

And suddenly Elsa's eyes sprang open. 'Now here's the really shocking news. Have you any idea where the centre of all this deadly activity is?'

'Not here,' gasped Tallulah excitedly.

'This area,' said Elsa, 'just sings with vampire activity – or it will soon.'

I raised my eyebrows in a highly sceptical way. But Tallulah was getting as excited as old Elsa. 'And these attacks at Brent Woods, they've got to be vampires too,' said Tallulah, who looked as if she'd just discovered she'd won a million pounds.

'Oh yes,' said Elsa. 'The leader has been experimenting to see what benefits human blood can bring. I believe he will conduct more experiments and then . . .' She sighed heavily. 'Well, I don't even want to think about an army of super-vampires, all here in Great Walden.'

'But hang on, Elsa,' I said. 'There's no actual proof those attacks in Brent Woods were made by a vampire. I mean, the victims didn't have any marks on their necks.'

'Didn't they?' cried Elsa. 'If they'd been examined by someone who'd studied vampires for years, like my Fergus, he would have found something for certain. Well, he predicted all this, you know. He actually said that the leader of these deadly vampires would arrive here, and start his attacks in Brent Woods. He even worked out the area he would move into. He said a house near the river. Vampires normally avoid running water. But this super-vampire wanted to show he's different.'

And then she showed us both an incredibly badly drawn map, with all four of the main roads around the river marked up. 'I haven't put in my road as I would have sensed if a vampire was as close to me as that,' said Elsa. 'But the vampire has lately moved into one of those other four roads for certain.'

'I don't suppose I could have this map?' asked Tallulah eagerly.

Elsa considered for a moment and then cried impulsively, 'All right, but please look after it, it's my only copy. My husband put in so much work on this, researching it for years. He tried to warn people, but no one listened. And now he's gone, and so it's up to me to complete his work and track down the leader of these super-vampires. That is why I rented this cottage. But . . .' She hesitated for a moment.

'Go on,' urged Tallulah.

'Well, the moment I moved here and started my investigations, things began happening to me.'

48

'What sort of things?' I asked.

'Accidents,' said Elsa grimly. 'I had so many accidents. Put them down to old age, if you like – but *I* think the vampires are on to me. And now I'm virtually housebound, or cottagebound to be strictly accurate. But I'm not giving up.' I couldn't help feeling impressed, even if it was a totally crazy mission.

She tottered to her feet and handed Tallulah the map.

'Thank you,' said Tallulah. 'I will look after it really carefully.'

'I have something else here to assist you.' Moving slowly with her stick, Elsa went over to a small desk.

'Can I help you . . . ?' I began.

'No thank you, dear, I know exactly where it is.' She opened the first drawer, and for a mad moment I thought she was going to offer us a gun. But instead, she held up a gold chain.

'One of my husband's most valuable possessions – oh, not valuable in terms of money but in what it can do. If ever you are near a vampire, this chain will, within seconds, become scorching hot. It's the best vampire-detector I've ever seen.'

She presented it to me. But I had a sudden fear that the gold chain might react to half-vampires too. So I swerved right away from it and said, 'No, Tallulah is the leader of this merry expedition.'

Of course, Tallulah pounced on the gold chain and was for once practically gushing. 'But this is wicked, brilliant. Are you sure you can spare it?'

'Oh yes,' said Elsa. 'What good is it locked away in a drawer? No, you use it, my dear, but please be very careful. The thing to remember about deadly vampires is that they are utterly ruthless. Nothing and no one must stand in their way. So I've got one very important piece of advice for you. If you should locate the vampire leader, whatever you do, don't look directly into his eyes.'

'In case he hypnotizes us, you mean?'

'He may do that,' said Elsa, 'but much more likely . . .' She hesitated for a moment. 'Well, if you let him, a vampire will try and get right inside your head and pick things up from you, such as your secret nightmares.

And then he will use this information – to torment you.'

And suddenly I was filled with terror. For I had a really terrible nightmare which had just followed me about for years. It always started with me lying in bed, then feeling this totally massive spider climbing up my body. It'd go scuttling over my arms, legs, face. And I could never stop it, so in the end it did something so horrible I don't even want to write it down. I'll just tell you that I'd wake up shaking all over.

But those nightmares are long gone now and could never return. I kept telling myself that until I noticed Elsa looking at me very anxiously. 'Are you all right, my dear?'

'Oh yeah,' I began in a low, trembling voice. I swallowed hard. 'Never better, in fact.'

But Elsa went on looking right at me as she said, 'Do not forget what I'm telling you. Never look straight into a vampire's eyes.'

'And Elsa, when we find this vampire—' said Tallulah impatiently.

'I wouldn't trust such vital information to the email or phone, or even to your wonderful website, so please come and tell me here.'

'But what . . . ?' I began. Then I hesitated, worried my question might sound rude.

But Elsa nodded. 'What can I, a very ancient lady indeed, do against a vampire? Well, never forget, all vampires live by a creed which can be summed up in four words: *pride lost – all lost.* So if we mere humans uncover their secret identity, the humiliation will be too much for them to bear and they'll vanish for a very long time, at least.' She smiled suddenly. 'And if we achieve that, we'll have saved the entire human race from something very dangerous indeed.'

CHAPTER SEVEN

Monday 5 November

6.05 p.m.

As soon as we'd left the cottage I said, 'You've got to admit it, old Elsa is a brilliant actress. In fact, I think they should let her have her own TV series. She really had me going for a few seconds there. How about you?'

Tallulah looked away from me and then said softly, 'I believe every word she said.'

'You're joking.'

'No.'

'So a lonely old lady gives you a map, which could have been scribbled by a three-year-old, and a gold chain she probably won at the fair, and tells you a load of nonsense about deadly vampires, who probably don't even exist.'

'It's not nonsense. What about those attacks in Brent Woods?' cried Tallulah.

'What about them?' I said. 'There's no proof at all they were made by vampires.'

'But no proof they weren't,' she said. Then she added, 'You don't want it to be true, do you?'

I had to admit it, Tallulah had scored a bull's-eye there. I really *didn't* want it to be true. Wasn't my life complicated enough, without tracking down some highly unpleasant relatives?

'Well, I'm really going to show you,' went on Tallulah. 'I know Elsa is genuine and I'll find this super-vampire. But don't worry, you run off and find a girl to go to the cinema with you; a girl who'll spend all her time talking about make-up and boy bands. I've got much more important things to do.'

Then she started walking away from me. In her eyes I was out of this adventure. And I didn't want that. I really didn't want to find a super-vampire either. But I had to follow this through, and know for certain that Elsa was talking sensational rubbish.

So I called after Tallulah, 'Do you ever watch *Doctor Who*?'

She stopped and whirled round. 'What!'

I said it again while walking towards her. 'Do you ever watch *Doctor Who*?'

'Of course I do.'

'Well, he investigates mysteries all over the universe, but he never goes alone. He always has a companion. I'll be that. I'll be your K-Nine. Now there's an offer you can't refuse.'

Tallulah considered for a moment. 'You may assist me then,' she said.

'Hey, thanks, I'm so honoured.'

'Meet me straight after school tomorrow. I shall have thought up a major plan of action then. Oh, and by the way . . .'

'Yes,' I said.

'I'm still not going to the cinema with you this Friday – or any other Friday either.'

She couldn't stop going on about that. She really was the rudest, most vampire-obsessed girl I'd ever met.

'Well, that's great,' I said, 'because I've already found someone else. She's incredibly beautiful too and said yes right after I asked her.'

That stopped Tallulah in her tracks for a second or two. But then she just muttered, 'Don't be late tomorrow as I won't wait for you,' and half ran away. While I went off triumphantly until I remembered I hadn't actually got a date for this Friday.

11.15 p.m.

Mum and Dad said I can have a break from flitting tonight. Good news, I suppose . . .

11.40 p.m.

I came downstairs to find Dad reading the local paper and Mum peering at the front page over his shoulder. She was murmuring something about it too. So I took a peek.

It was about the attacks in Brent Woods: WHAT KIND OF ANIMAL IS IT? And underneath, this guy who'd been attacked said: *'I'm sure it wasn't a human. It was some kind of wild creature that just tore at me.'*

'You don't suppose this animal could be a vampire, do you?'

Dad jumped forward in his chair, as if I'd

just given him an electric shock. And Mum let out a deep sigh. 'Now, whatever made you say that, Marcus?' she demanded.

'Well, it could be, couldn't it? Maybe a breakaway group of vampires who *do* like human blood or what it does to them? And I just wondered if you had any inside information about this. After all, we are related to them.'

'No, we're not,' Mum and Dad shouted together.

'Oh, I thought vampires were our cousins or second cousins or eighth-removed or something.'

'Please keep your voice down when discussing matters such as this,' said Dad, even though he was shouting himself. 'And remember, we *half*-vampires are ordinary people who just happen to have extraordinary powers and gifts, which we use carefully and for the good of all. While vampires are . . .' He hesitated suddenly.

'Monsters,' I prompted.

'Something completely different to us,' said Dad. 'They leave us alone on the condition that we leave them completely alone.'

'It's fine to read about them in books,' Mum went on, 'but in real life they are to be avoided at all times. Is that clear?'

I nodded, figuring this probably wasn't the moment to tell them I was going vampire hunting with Tallulah tomorrow.

The Vampira Website

A highly important message to all from Vampira:
Don't bother to send me any more messages because I am now closing down this site. This is partly because of the low quality of most of the stuff you've sent me, but mainly because I'm off on a important mission which I cannot tell a single human about.

Soon I will be able to prove for certain that vampires exist. Sorry, but I daren't tell you any more. This mission is just so important.

Keep believing in vampires, though.

CHAPTER EIGHT

Tuesday 6 November

9.00 a.m.

'It was really tough, but I've done it,' announced Joel at school today.

'Done what?'

'Found a girl who doesn't find you completely repulsive. She saw you at the firework party last Friday and only threw up a little bit. And she will go with you to the cinema on Friday night – chaperoned by Katie and me, of course.'

'So who is this girl with such amazing good taste?' I asked.

'Her name is Julie and Katie says she's lovely.'

'Which usually means the total opposite. And I don't remember her at the firework party.'

'Neither do I,' Joel admitted. 'But it was crammed with people, so that doesn't mean anything.'

I hesitated for a moment.

'Come on, Marcus, I'll bet she'll be a lot more fun than Tallulah. So are you up for it?'

I grinned. 'Why not?'

'Great, you won't regret it,' said Joel. 'Well, you might, but it'll be a laugh anyway.'

4.05 p.m.

It's a grey drizzly afternoon and Tallulah and I have already sped through Brent Woods and are now at the top of Priestly Drive, poring over this so-called vampire map. According to Elsa, this super-vampire resides on one of four roads.

'So what's our plan, O great one?' I asked.

'If you're going to be silly, you can go home,' said Tallulah.

'What! I only asked what our plan was.'

'We will stroll up and down the roads marked on this vampire map, looking for anyone the least bit suspicious-looking. The moment we spot them we'll wave the vampire detection chain in their direction.'

Well, I was waiting for more – much more.

But Tallulah stopped there. So that was it. Her master plan. I tell you, I nearly burst out laughing. I mean, for a start, who says vampires are going to stalk about in a suspicious manner anyway? Surely vampires – like half-vampires – will have learned how to blend in and not draw attention to themselves. So you could say a vampire will probably be the *least* suspicious-looking person we meet.

And then it's all so random. How do we know a vampire is going to be roaming about now? He or she might not come out until eleven o'clock tonight.

I'd actually been a bit apprehensive – even a little nervous – about this vampire quest. But now I'm convinced it's going to be a total disaster.

And I can just relax and enjoy myself.

4.10 p.m.
Tallulah has just charged over to this huge

man who bears an uncanny resemblance to a gorilla. She walked right into him, while whirling her chain about.

'Young lady, please watch where you are going,' he rumbled. Tallulah didn't bother to answer. She just went on staring sternly at the chain. 'Whatever happened to good manners?' the man moaned, while Tallulah continued to ignore him.

Then she stomped away dejectedly and hissed, 'Not even a little bit warm. And I had such high hopes of him.'

4.20 p.m.

'Tallulah, here's a little tip for you,' I say. 'When you find someone who looks at all suspicious, don't wave the chain right in front of their face. First of all, if it is a vampire, they'll know you're on to them. And secondly, they may well shout at you for some time . . . as that last man did.'

Tallulah glares at me. 'If you say one more smug thing like that, I'll punch you.'

4.25 p.m.

Every single person we passed, Tallulah

suspected. And each time she swung that chain about madly – with absolutely no results at all.

I wondered suddenly if Elsa and all her cats were killing themselves laughing as we trailed hopelessly about in the rain, clutching a chain which probably had no special powers at all.

But no, I don't think Elsa is laughing at us. She's just a charming nutcase. Well, that's OK with me. The last thing I want is to start tracking down vampires. My parents are right on this one thing: I should keep totally away from them.

And yet, I couldn't let Tallulah do this on her own. For some mad reason I had to be part of it.

5.20 p.m.

It's raining hard now and I murmured, 'We should have brought an umbrella.'

'Don't be so wet.'

'Hey, you made a joke – sort of. Your first, I think.' Then I added, 'Shall we just stop and take shelter somewhere?'

'Why?'

'Well, I don't really see the point of just walking up and down these roads for hours and hours.'

'Have you got a better idea?' she demanded.

'Well, yes, I have, actually. Elsa reckons this vampire only came to the area very recently. Why don't we ask at that newsagent's at the bottom of Croft Avenue if anyone new has moved in lately? We'll have to think up a reason why we want to know—'

'That's a really good idea,' interrupted Tallulah disbelievingly.

'Don't sound so shocked. I do get good ideas occasionally.'

'We'll do it,' said Tallulah, 'just after we've tested *him*.'

She pointed at an odd-looking guy in a pinstriped suit, who was marching along Priestly Drive at a furious pace under an umbrella. He came up right beside me and quickly sped off.

Then Tallulah gave a little cry of amazement and gasped, 'Marcus, the chain has turned red-hot!'

CHAPTER NINE

Tuesday 6 November

6.00 p.m.

Tallulah handed the chain over to me very solemnly. I reached out and touched it and said, 'It's a bit warm, I suppose.'

'But it was freezing cold just a few seconds before. The temperature has definitely changed.'

'Yeah, but aren't vampires supposed to turn this chain red-hot?'

'We only saw him for a few seconds though,' said Tallulah. 'If he hadn't dashed off, it would probably have been boiling by now. Come on, we mustn't let him get away from us.'

I strongly suspected we were chasing an innocent man, but before I could say anything a voice called out, 'Tallulah! Tallulah! Over here.'

Tallulah looked round, then froze in horror for a moment before saying, 'Just ignore her, keep going.'

'But who is it?'

'The local madwoman.'

'What!'

'Also known as my mum.' Then Tallulah added, 'She got all worked up because I was home so late yesterday and made me promise I'd come straight home today. Of course, that's the last thing I can do. Oh, I don't believe it,' she added as the 'local madwoman' came charging up towards us.

'Tallulah,' she called, and then, after peering at me for a moment, 'It is Marcus, isn't it?'

'The very same,' I said cheerfully.

'But what are you doing running about in the rain? You're both soaked through.'

'Oh, is it raining?' I said. 'We hadn't noticed, we were just so busy, er . . . walking about.'

'Your father's waiting in the car,' Tallulah's mum went on. 'You know what he said to you yesterday.' Whatever it was, it was enough for Tallulah to lower her head and groan loudly.

'Can we give you a lift home, Marcus?' asked her mum.

I was about to say yes when Tallulah looked up and mouthed at me, 'Follow that vampire.'

So I replied, 'No, it's OK thanks, I've got to do some stuff,' and then I sped off while Tallulah was half dragged into a waiting car. At first, I couldn't find the pinstriped guy at all. But finally I located him right at the top of Priestly Drive, one of the roads marked on Elsa's map.

He was standing outside a small house, still under the umbrella but stroking his chin, as if he were trying to remember something – maybe it was where he'd put his keys. He was wearing expensive-looking gloves and had glasses on a chain around his neck. He had a small pointy beard and a catastrophic nose. I'd guess his age was about fifty – maybe even older.

Having found out where he lived, I was about to speed past him and go home when he called out, 'Rotten night, isn't it?'

For a moment I couldn't believe he was talking to me and looked around to see if someone else had popped up. But we were quite alone.

'That's the trouble with this climate, isn't it? You never know where you are with it, changes all the time,' he continued. 'Have you got far to go?'

'No, not very far,' I replied cautiously.

'Because I can always lend you my umbrella – no hurry about returning it either, just the next time you're in the area.'

I gaped at him. He was being so incredibly friendly he was starting to freak me out.

Then I remembered something Elsa said: *Never look directly at a vampire.* Yet that's exactly what I'd just been doing. Is that why he'd been chatting to me? He'd seen the chain, recognized it as a vampire detector and now . . . What total, total rubbish. He was just a nice guy, trying to be helpful.

'Thanks for the offer,' I said, 'but the rain doesn't bother me. See you then.'

7.05 p.m.

I'm very ashamed of myself. For two whole seconds I wondered if Mr Pinstripe was a super-vampire. It just shows how you can be infected by the maddest ideas. I still think Elsa won that mangy chain at the fair. And Tallulah and I have just been racing about on the stupidest mission ever.

7.45 p.m.

I was just finishing my tea when my parents came into the room, smiling. This immediately filled me with alarm.

'We've decided you can have another break from flitting tonight,' said Mum.

It's weird; I want them to get off my case, yet I feel disappointed when they do.

'We'd also like you to do us a favour,' said Mum. 'There is a half-vampire of your age who hasn't changed over yet and is having a few problems.'

'Poor guy,' I murmured. He was probably just happily going about his life when *whizz-bang*, on the night of his thirteenth birthday, he gets news which just changes everything for ever. I knew exactly how he was feeling.

'We thought you might be able to help,' went on Mum.

'Me?!' I'm amazed. 'Yeah, OK, I'll talk to him.'

'It's a girl, actually,' said Dad.

'A girl! Hey, you don't think of girls being half-vampires, do you? Well, I know you're one, Mum, but you changed over during the Iron Age, didn't you? It's just weird to think of a modern girl turning into a half-vampire, isn't it?'

'Not at all,' said Mum briskly. 'It will be a wonderful moment in her life.'

'And meeting me will be another wonderful moment in her life. OK, I'll see her – and give her the low-down on being a half-vampire.'

A flicker of doubt crossed Mum's face then. 'I know you'll do your best to be really positive and help her,' she said. 'I'll call her mum now and fix a time. Thursday, I think.'

9.15 p.m.

At last, Tallulah rang me.

'I can't talk for long,' she said, and her voice sounded hoarse and croaky.

'Are you all right?' I asked.

71

'Never better.'

'Did your parents give you a hard time?'

'Oh, I can handle them,' she said. 'Tell me what happened then.'

I did, and I could practically hear her listening. She was just devouring my every word. Then she cried, 'You didn't let him look directly at you, did you?'

'Well, just for a bit, but he probably didn't see me that clearly, with all that rain and everything. And look, Mr Pinstripe is not a vampire.'

'Why did the chain turn hot then?' demanded Tallulah.

'It didn't – it just went a bit warm.'

'But why did it do that?'

'I don't know, maybe it suddenly got a suntan. But that doesn't prove anything.'

'Yes it does, and tomorrow I want you to find out if Mr Pinstripe has moved in recently. You could ask that newsagent.'

'Excuse me, but whose idea was that in the first place?'

She ignored this and said, 'Then try and see Mr Pinstripe again. He might be roaming about the same time as yesterday. If he is,

engage him in conversation – without looking
directly at him, of course. I'm going to let you
borrow the chain, and if it turns red-hot this
time – well, we'll know for certain we've
found our vampire, which will be fantastic.'

'Just one question: where will you be when
I'm doing all this?'

'I've got to go straight home tomorrow and
see someone I really don't want to see, but I
can't get out of it.'

'Highly mysterious,' I said.

'Not at all, it's deeply boring, actually, but
my parents are coming to school to fetch
me. They're determined I won't miss this
person. But that's not important because I
believe you can do this mission on your own
tomorrow. I've got complete confidence in
you.'

'Have you really?' I asked.

'No, but I thought I'd better pretend I had.
But if you do track down this vampire
tomorrow . . .'

'Yes . . .'

'I'll realize you're not the total idiot I
thought you were. So try not to let me
down.'

11.55 p.m.

'Try not to let me down!' Talk about cheeky, and I love the way I've ended up doing all the work tomorrow. Still, that's girls for you! Been thinking about girls a lot tonight, actually. There's this half-vampire girl I'm going to meet on Thursday, my blind date, Julie, on Friday, and then there's Tallulah, of course . . . Yeah, always Tallulah.

Wednesday 7 November

2.50 a.m.

Something truly bad has just happened.

I woke up to find something crawling up my body. I could actually feel it scuttling about. Its legs even tickled slightly. And although I couldn't see it, I knew exactly what it was: a whacking great spider.

Then it slid right onto my face. I wanted to yell out, scream, jump up and fling this thing off me. But I wasn't able to do any of those things. I was paralysed with terror. So I was unable to stop that spider from slowly, steadily, eating my face.

I just had to lie there while it ate me alive. Soon all that would be left of me was a rotting skeleton.

Bit of a shock for my mum in the morning, wondering why I wasn't getting ready for school. She'd pull back the covers of my bed and find the remains of her son. 'So that's why he's not up and dressed,' she'd say.

Yeah, OK, it was a nightmare: my worst-ever nightmare, which always scared me witless. Yet it had left me alone for ages and ages. Only tonight it was back. Why?

It must have been because I'd thought about it earlier. There was no other reason. Only actually, there was.

2.59 a.m

If you let him, a vampire will try and get right inside your head and pick things up from you, such as your secret nightmares. And then they will use this information – to torment you.

3.02 a.m.

That's not what happened tonight. No way.

3.04 a.m.

Just a very weird coincidence. Well, life is packed full of them. And this was just another one.

CHAPTER TEN

Wednesday 7 November

7.00 a.m.
Kept waking up. In fact, I probably slept for no more than an hour last night. And even us half-vampires need more sleep than that. I am certain Mr Pinstripe is not a vampire. But even so I'm going straight home tonight. Tallulah will not be very pleased when I tell her.

12.30 p.m.
I haven't told Tallulah yet. Well, she was late and now she's been sent to Townley, our extremely grim headmaster. She's been gone for ages as well. What can she be in trouble for now?

3.30 p.m.

It wasn't until the end of school that I finally saw Tallulah at the gate. And she looked incredibly tired. I bet she'd been up all night rowing with her parents. That wouldn't surprise me.

'So what did Townley want to see you about?' I asked.

'Oh, the usual rubbish,' she said dismissively. 'He's not important. This is.' And she handed me a carrier bag. 'I wouldn't trust anyone in the world with this but you,' she said, and then added, 'Oh no, here comes my mum already. Got to go. Very best of luck, Marcus.' And with that she was gone.

There inside the bag was the very precious (in her opinion) or totally worthless (in my opinion) chain. And I didn't say any of the stuff I meant to say. It was because of Tallulah saying, *I wouldn't trust anyone in the world with this but you.* That caught me unawares – and by the time I'd recovered from the shock, she'd gone.

3.45 p.m.

I've decided I will drop into the newsagent's

in Croft Avenue and find out if anyone new has moved in lately. But after I've done that I'll go straight home.

4.30 p.m.

As I strolled into the newsagent's at the bottom of Croft Avenue, the woman behind the counter glared very suspiciously at me and demanded, 'Yes, what do you want?'

She wasn't the apple-cheeked, brimming-with-friendliness person I was hoping to find there. Still, I'd win her over. So I greeted her like a long-lost relative: 'Oh hi, how are you? I'm here to ask you a massive favour.'

'We don't do credit,' she snapped, 'especially to school children.'

'Oh, it's nothing like that,' I said, grinning like crazy. 'I'm doing a project for school, where I have to interview people about their life and experiences. Important local people' – I paused – 'like you.'

Seconds later she was eating out of my hand, babbling away about . . . her marriage, her time in local government . . . And I had to listen to all this without going into a coma. But I knew I couldn't blurt my question out right away, it would have just made her suspicious. So I pretended to scribble down everything she said in my notebook.

Then I asked about her customers in Priestly Drive. And finally – FINALLY – came my killer question. 'So have you had any new people move into Priestly Drive recently?'

'Just the one,' she said, 'and at number one, actually.'

Then I asked, coaxingly, 'I bet you don't know his name?'

'I certainly do,' she began, but then she broke off and laughed as the shop door opened. 'We've just been talking about you,' she cried.

And there, standing in the doorway . . . was Mr Pinstripe.

CHAPTER ELEVEN

Wednesday 7 November

5.30 p.m.

'Now, I always fear the worst when people say they've been talking about me,' he said. 'A guilty conscience, you might say.' But he didn't look very worried as he strode up to the counter. He was in his pinstriped suit again. 'So, to put me out of my misery, what am I in trouble for?'

'Oh, Giles,' laughed the woman behind the counter, who was clearly his biggest fan. 'Don't worry, it's just this young man here is doing a project and has been asking me all sorts of questions about my life.' She couldn't help a note of pride entering her voice as she

81

said this. 'And he was just asking about new customers when you walked in.'

Giles glanced at me. 'Ah, we had a brief chat in the rain yesterday, didn't we? Well, I'm a very new and very satisfied customer. This wonderful lady has even ordered in a magazine especially for me.'

'And it arrived this morning too,' she said, and scurried off to get it.

Giles turned his attention to me. My eyes instantly slid away from him and onto my notebook. 'Actually, could I ask you a couple of questions?'

'Oh, have you finished with me?' said the shopkeeper, returning with the magazine and sounding disappointed.

'For now, yes,' I said. 'You've been brilliantly helpful.'

'She always is,' said Giles. 'And I shall devour this from cover to cover,' he added, slipping his magazine, which was about stamp collecting, into his briefcase.

The way he'd used the word *devour* – was that a secret code to his vampire nature? No, no, no, of course not.

'Been mad about stamps ever since I was a

boy,' he went on. 'The hobbies which nourish us then never quite leave us, do they?'

Wasn't *nourish* a sort of vampire word too? No, I had to stop doing this. Mr Pinstripe was just trying to be friendly and funny. Too hard – perhaps that's why everything he said sounded a bit forced and smarmy.

'Thank you again, my dear,' he said to the shopkeeper. He turned to me. 'Now, I'm in rather a rush but I always like to assist young people. Let's talk outside, shall we?'

Out on the street, I reached for the chain with my right hand while trying to hold my notebook with my left hand. I decided I might as well check out the chain while I was here. Not that I was expecting anything at all. 'Well, the first question I'd like to ask you,' I said, 'is: what's your name?'

'Giles Wallace,' he said. 'And now I know I've got at least one right.' He smiled, showing a definite gap between his two front teeth. I was swinging that chain about in my right pocket. It was definitely getting a bit warmer, but nowhere near scalding hot, as Elsa had predicted. Maybe it needed to be held closer to him. So I very carefully eased the chain out of my pocket.

'Could I also ask you why you moved here?'

'That's an easy one. I've wanted to return to this part of the country for a while. I knew it well once, long ago – before you were even thought of, in fact. And now, finally, I've managed it.'

I was edging the chain even closer to him when he demanded, 'But what's this then?' And he said it so suddenly that I lost my grip on the chain and sent it flying onto the ground. He swooped on it in an instant. 'This looks highly unusual.' His small gloved hands were all over it. 'Is it a present?'

'Yeah, that's right, only it doesn't actually belong to me,' I said, getting very confused. 'It belongs to a girl I know and I'm just looking after it for her.' That sounded so feeble, I added, 'It's a bit broken so I'm going to try and mend it for her.' Then I practically snatched it back from him.

'Well, it looks as if it might be very valuable, so take good care of it, won't you?'

I could barely answer him. I was still too shocked at the way he'd just leaped onto my chain, as if he had a right to examine it. 'So do you live near here?' he asked.

And I blurted out. 'Yeah, number nine Drake Drive.'

'The other side of the village, then,' he said. He sounded surprised while I wondered why on earth I'd just blabbed my address out like that. 'I must go now,' he said. 'But we'll meet again, I'm sure, and next time I shall have some questions for you!'

7.20 p.m.

I told Tallulah everything. 'Tomorrow I'll trail Giles,' she said, then added, 'It's probably better if you don't come with me tomorrow.'

I hesitated. 'Well . . .'

'No, honestly, I want to be totally inconspicuous.'

That was something I couldn't picture at all.

'And if he sees you there again he might get suspicious. Especially as he knows you don't live anywhere near there.' I felt as if I'd messed this mission up, dropping the chain and blurting out my address. But then Tallulah added unexpectedly, 'You haven't done so very badly.'

85

Thursday 8 November

3.40 a.m.

The spider of death was back in my dream and scuttling all over me again. Only tonight something incredible happened. After a bit, I could move. So I leaped out of my bed. But somehow I couldn't shake that spider off me. And I could feel its legs clinging so tightly onto me. So I raised my hand, determined to push it off. But then I decided if I did that it would still be in my bedroom, ready to creep back onto me again. Ready to eat me alive, when I least expected it.

So instead I found a hankie in my trouser pocket, reached forward and somehow scooped the spider up into it. I nearly dropped the hankie again as I felt its legs twitching and turning about inside the hankie.

But somehow I yanked open my bedroom window and hurled the hankie and spider outside. After which I crumpled onto my bed, totally exhausted – but triumphant.

A few moments later I woke up to find my bedroom freezing cold. Then I realized my bedroom window was swinging open. That dream must have seemed so real I'd actually opened the window. And maybe one of my stinky hankies was also lying on the front lawn. That made me smile.

But still, I'd done it, hadn't I? Somehow I'd managed to overcome my fear and fling the spider away. I'd never done that before.

4.05 a.m.

Does this mean that dream won't bother me again? Not now I'd beaten it. I hope so.

7.10 a.m.

I was just getting dressed for school when I casually reached into my school trouser pocket for the chain. I kept it there as I didn't want my parents spotting it and bombarding me with questions about it. They might even know what it is.

Only it's not there any more.

It's gone.

CHAPTER TWELVE

Thursday 8 November

7.25 a.m.
I must have hidden the chain away in my bedroom after all. Anyway, it's got to be here.

7.40 a.m.
Only it isn't. I've searched everywhere. But it can't have just melted away in the night. That's impossible.

7.41 a.m.
Unless . . .

7.42 a.m.
Unless when I was sleepwalking and dug into

my trouser pocket last night, it wasn't a hankie I pulled out. It was the chain. And then I flung the chain out of the window and into my front garden, where no doubt the vampire was waiting. And it wouldn't have taken him any time at all to hastily pocket it and slip away.

And who is the vampire?

The man who looked like a gorilla?

That very angry woman who shouted at Tallulah?

Or Giles?

Giles, who stopped and talked to me long enough to pick up my nightmares. Giles, who actually knows where I live. No, he's got to be suspect number one. And now he could have the chain, thanks to me – the Vampire's Apprentice – throwing it down to him.

So what has Giles got lined up for me tonight? Maybe he'll get me to sleepwalk out of my house and perform a burglary.

7.44 a.m.

Hey listen, blog, I'm going seriously nutty. I mean, all that stuff I just wrote. What actual proof have I got that Giles is a vampire, apart from that mind-blowingly pathetic chain?

My entire proof is that Giles stopped and chatted to me in the rain and said *'devour'* in a way that reminded me of a vampire.

Pathetic!

7.47 a.m.
So just one small question then – where is my chain?

8.03 a.m.
I sat eating my breakfast without tasting a morsel of it. Then Mum said, 'Don't forget, we're going to see Gracie tonight.'

'Who's Gracie?' I murmured.

'Oh, Marcus,' said Mum, 'she's this girl who's just discovered she's a half-vampire. We thought you could help her . . .'

Oh yeah, yeah, yeah,' I said, still far away. 'I'll do that.'

'And I keep forgetting to sew up that hole in your trouser pocket. Now it's up to you to remind me, Marcus. For now, remember to put your medicine in the other pocket, won't you?'

For a moment I couldn't reply; I just went on staring at Mum until I burst out, 'There's a hole in my left pocket, isn't there?' Then I started to laugh. 'But that's brilliant, fantastic news. I'm so happy.'

Mum was staring at me now in considerable alarm. 'Are you feeling quite well?'

'Never better, Mum.' I grinned. 'Thanks to you.' Of course, of course, I'd been keeping the chain in my right pocket because there's a hole in my left. But after I'd snatched the chain back from Giles, I could easily have forgotten and put it in the wrong pocket. And it probably slipped out on my way home and is lying on a path somewhere at this very moment.

9.30 a.m.

I'm not at school yet. Instead, I'm still searching for the chain. I haven't found it yet, but I'll have another big hunt tonight. And I will track it down or my name's not Marcus Howlett – which it undoubtedly is.

11.00 a.m.

Break time, and the moment I'd been

dreading: telling Tallulah about the chain. She gave a great hacking cough first.

'You sound awful.'

'And you look awful,' she said.

I smiled. 'That time at charm school is really paying off, isn't it?'

'I'll have the chain back now,' she announced.

'There's just one very small problem about that,' I said. Tallulah's eyes were boring into me now. 'I've very temporarily mislaid it.'

'Stop joking,' she growled, 'and hand it over.'

'It must have fallen out of my pocket last night. There's this dirty great hole there and that's what's happened,' I said confidently. It was the only explanation which made any sense. And I didn't want to spend a second thinking about any others. 'But fear not, I will have the most wide-ranging search in the history of mankind and womankind after school and track it down without fail.'

Tallulah was trying to say something and I don't think it was, 'Well done,' but instead she had another coughing fit. Then she managed to splutter, 'We've got to find it.'

'And we will. But meanwhile, go and take

a bucket of medicine or something. I'm worried about you.'

'Just worry about that chain,' she snapped.

2.45 p.m.
Tallulah had a major coughing fit at the end of morning school. She was sent to our fearsome matron and never returned. I've just found out that Tallulah has been sent home. I'm not surprised – and more than a bit relieved as well. For it means I can now search for that chain after school without Tallulah snarling at me all the time.

4.55 p.m.
There isn't a speck of land between my house and Priestly Drive which has not been scrutinized by me. And I still haven't found that chain.

I even went into that newsagent's again to see if anyone had handed it in. The woman there greeted me like an old friend and was ready to tell me more fascinating tales from her life, but she didn't know anything about the chain. She said someone could have just picked it up.

And that's what happened. Got to be.

5.45 p.m.

'I know you'll be tactful tonight when you see Gracie,' said my mum, 'as when a girl turns into a half-vampire she has one or two extra changes. So just after her fang appeared, Gracie's face became lightly covered with hair.'

'Like a werewolf?' I said.

'No, nothing like a werewolf,' said Mum sharply. 'And please don't ever make that comparison again. The hair will disappear – eventually. But Gracie is a little distressed by the whole experience.'

'And you don't want me to burst in and say, 'Hi, hairy, didn't I see you in a film once? *Killer Werewolves*, I think it was call—'

'Actually,' interrupted Mum, 'I'd much rather you didn't mention her extra hair growth at all.'

'Pretend I hadn't noticed it, you mean.'

'I think that would be best,' said Mum.

'Bit unlikely though, isn't it?' I said. 'Unless I say I'm very short-sighted. That's it – and my glasses have been smashed.'

'I'll just remind you that this is a fellow half-vampire who needs a bit of cheering up,' hissed Mum. Then her eyes narrowed as she added, 'I know you won't let her – or us – down.'

8.25 p.m.

Gracie lived about five miles away with her mum (her dad died in a car accident a few years ago). My parents had met Gracie's mum at a secret meeting for half-vampires whose children were 'about to change over'.

'So we don't know her very well,' said Mum with a nervous gulp. She gave another nervous gulp when we arrived: the house was in total darkness.

'Are you sure they're expecting us?' I asked.

'Oh yes,' said Mum, while looking at Dad.

Mum rang the doorbell twice. Then a voice hissed, 'Look, I've got to switch the light on to answer the door.'

One dim light went on, the door opened and there was, I assumed, Gracie's mum. She announced, 'You're all going to wish you'd stayed at home. What a carry-on we're having here tonight! Girls all take the facial hair so badly.'

Well, you couldn't really blame them for that, I thought.

'I try and tell her it's just a phase,' went on Gracie's mum, 'and that I've been through it and lived to tell the tale. Only that doesn't cheer her up at all, because I'm old and so I haven't a clue about anything. Oh, she's driven me to distraction today, especially as she was so hoping to be in the school play. And it's the auditions this very week. Of course, there's absolutely no way she can go along, and that is a shame – as she'd set her heart on it.'

'Is she good at acting then?' I asked.

'Oh yes, wonderful . . .' began Gracie's mum, and then she looked at me as if noticing me for the first time. 'Do you know, I think it might be best if you saw Gracie on your own, if that's all right?'

Mum and Dad weren't at all sure about me visiting Gracie alone. They were worried I was about to make things even worse.

'Perhaps if I come too?' said Mum.

'No, you're all right, Mum,' I said. 'So where is Gracie lurking then?'

Before Gracie's mum could reply, a voice shrieked, 'I don't want to talk to anyone. Just tell them all to go home.'

'But I know she'd like to see another young person. Well, she might,' added Gracie's mum a little less certainly. 'Anyway, she's upstairs, the last door on the right.'

The stairs were in darkness; so was the landing. But I stumbled over to the final door on the right and knocked lightly. There was no answer. I knocked a bit louder. Silence again. So then I pushed open the door. The room was pitch-dark too, but I could just make out someone sitting on the bed in the corner.

Suddenly she whispered, 'If you switch on any lights you're going to regret it.'

I didn't switch on any lights.

Then she added, 'I ought to be in the circus. *Come and see the Bearded Schoolgirl.* I'd be the star attraction.'

'You definitely would. Can I be your manager?'

She peered at me. 'Come a bit closer.'

'OK.'

Hair had indeed sprouted all over her face. It wasn't massively thick, but it covered even her chin and forehead, and great big tufts of it hung down off her ears as well.

'I'm not even allowed to shave it,' she said.

'Why not?'

'It makes it grow even thicker for some reason. Don't ask me why. None of it makes any sense.'

I nodded in total agreement, then said quickly, 'But it won't last.'

'I'll always be a half-vampire, though. I'll always be a weirdo.'

'Yeah, but in my opinion weird people are the only ones worth knowing.' I was making this up as I went along, but sort of believing it. 'I mean, if everyone was just ordinary then normal life would be so dull, the whole country would die of boredom. So really, you and I are helping to keep millions of people alive – think of that.'

She suddenly switched on her bedside lamp and stared at me. 'I was so sure you'd be ugly.'

'And instead . . . ?'

She sort of smiled. 'Stop fishing for compliments.'

And she wasn't exactly ugly either. Of course, all that facial hair wasn't a great look. But I could see she was really quite pretty, with long hair and large green eyes.

'Right now, I'm so hideous,' she cried. 'And if any of my so-called friends saw me, well, they'd either run from the room screaming or kill themselves laughing.'

'Or they'd get out their mobile phones and take a picture,' I said.

'Oh, a few of them would definitely do that and then post the pictures up on Facebook. I'd never be able to leave the house at all then.'

'So how long have you got to stay hidden away in here?'

'Oh, weeks and weeks yet.'

'Surely not for that long?'

'Yes, because although this hair will fall off in a few days, it might suddenly come back again – and without any warning either. So I could be sitting there in history my normal self one day, and the very next day I start turning back into the Bearded Girl.'

'It really could happen again as fast as that?'

'*Just while you're in your convalescence, my dear,*' said Gracie, doing a brilliant impersonation of her mum. I smiled, but then Gracie's voice rose. 'I've also got to look out for vampires, who just love my blood apparently. I don't suppose any vampires attacked you!'

She was expecting me to say, 'No, of course not,' and her eyes opened wide in horror when I said airily, 'Oh, just the one – twice.' And then I remembered I was supposed to be cheering her up. 'But I don't like to talk about that.' I sat down on the edge of the bed. 'And there is a good side to all this,' I said.

'Like what?' she demanded.

'Well, you won't need so much sleep, so you can stay up late.'

'I do, anyway.'

'And you'll learn how to turn into a bat.'

'Er, I loathe and detest bats. What else?'

'Well . . .'

'You can't think of anything else, can you?' she cried. 'And answer me this . . . if you had a choice: that you could be a half-vampire or be normal, which would it be?'

100

'Like I said, no one interesting is normal.'

'You haven't answered my question.' And she was staring right at me now.

'OK, when I found out I was a half-vampire I just freaked out. It was like everything I knew about myself had just slipped away. And my life tipped over into Weirdsville, where it's stayed ever since. And yeah, if I had a choice I'd rather not be a half-vampire. But I'll tell you this, deep down I'm still me, Marcus Howlett. By the way, have they tried to get you to change your name?'

Gracie nodded. 'My half-vampire name is Flame. I mean, what sort of name is that?'

'Definitely not yours,' I said firmly. 'Mine was supposed to be Jed or Ned – no, Ved, that's it. Ved the undead – I added that last bit. But what sort of name was that? Not mine.'

'So what did you do?' asked Gracie.

'Said my name is Marcus and nothing was going to change that. And in the end they had to give up.'

'So you won!' said Gracie.

I grinned. 'Yeah, I suppose I did. Do you want to be called Flame?'

'I loathe and detest that name.'

'Well, I'll help you stay Gracie too.'

'Thanks,' she said quietly. Then she suddenly got up. 'Come on.'

'Come on where?'

'Downstairs. I'm starving.'

Her mum gave a flutter of amazement when she saw Gracie downstairs, and eating too. ('Refused to eat anything all day,' she whispered to Mum.)

As I was leaving, Gracie gave me her text number. 'Us freaks have got to stick together,' she said.

9.35 p.m.

'Well done,' said Mum in the car home. 'I believe you've turned things round for Gracie tonight.'

'Told her about all the wonderful opportunities being a half-vampire can offer, did you?' asked Dad.

'Something like that,' I murmured.

10.05 p.m.

A text from Gracie:

For the past few days I've been hating every single bit of my life. I don't hate it quite so much now – thanks to you.

My reply:

Yeah, I rock. And if ever you feel depressed, get in contact. It'll probably make you feel even worse, but do it anyway. And never let anyone call you Flame – except me!

There was also a short message from Tallulah:

You'd better have found my chain.

My confident (!) reply:

Don't worry, I will. Hope your cough isn't too grisly.

Friday 9 November

6.50 a.m.

I fell asleep much quicker than I'd expected. Maybe it was seeing Gracie. She got me thinking about stuff other than disappearing chains and vampires.

But here's the really top news: no nightmares at all, or if I did have any, I can't remember them. Of course, you could say the vampire didn't need to send me any nightmares. Not now he has the chain.

But now I'm thinking total rubbish again.

For a start, if that chain's a genuine vampire detector, I'll change my name to Flame.

Do you want to know something else, blog? I'm sick of the whole thing: chains, supervampires, strange attacks in Brent Woods. Right now, I just want to float away from it all. That's why I'm declaring today a vampire-free zone. And instead, I'm going to totally concentrate on really important stuff.

Like my blind date tonight.

CHAPTER THIRTEEN

Friday 9 November

6.30 p.m.

Just spent a whole day at school without thinking about vampires once. Of course, I was greatly helped in this by the fact that Tallulah was still away. But when she does return I shall just tell her quite calmly and quietly that I am handing in my notice as a vampire watcher. Tallulah won't understand, as she's just insanely obsessed by vampires. But maybe if I stay away from her for a while she'll start to miss me.

To be honest, there's absolutely no chance of that happening. I've just got to accept that Tallulah and I have come to a dead end. But

I don't care. Well, I won't soon, as I'll be far too busy with my new girlfriend. Yeah, I know I'm jumping ahead here. But I've got a really good feeling about this date. And when Julie sees me with my hair all washed and teeth freshly brushed – well, who knows what could happen?

7.15 p.m.

Joel and I were waiting outside the cinema for our dates in a cool, confident way (my left knee was only shaking a bit).

I said, 'I just wish I could remember what Julie looks like.'

'She's hard to miss, actually,' replied Joel, 'as she's got this squint.'

That gave me a start. 'You never told me about that.'

'But don't worry; she doesn't squint all the time,' said Joel. 'There's the odd second when she stops.'

'Now you tell me,' I muttered.

'And her bad breath is nowhere near as foul as it used to be. As for that funny burping noise she keeps making . . .' Joel couldn't say any more, as I was too busy punching him. Then we both started laughing, but a bit too loudly, if you know what I mean.

Although I'd never dare say this aloud, tonight is my first proper date with a girl – and Joel's too. And we both so want it to be a success. That's why we kept messing about and laughing.

We were still laughing madly when the girls turned up.

'You two sound in a good mood,' says Katie.

Beside her was a small blonde girl who was introduced to me as Julie. She said softly, 'We met last Saturday but it was only for a second, so you've probably forgotten.'

'No, I remember it all right.' That was a lie but I was shocked at my very poor memory as she was extremely pretty. And I insisted on paying for her ticket and buying us some popcorn. No expense spared by me tonight.

Then Joel and Katie slipped on ahead of us. They'd already linked arms.

I smiled at Julie and – do you know? – she grinned right back, just as if she actually wanted to be going out with me, which was truly incredible.

And I just knew this was going to be a top night.

8.50 p.m.

No, it wasn't.

It was a total and complete *disaster*.

CHAPTER FOURTEEN

Friday 9 November

8.51 p.m.

Sitting in the back of the cinema with Julie, I had no idea of the terrible events which were about to unfold.

We'd let the girls choose the film: a dismal-sounding romantic comedy. But I didn't care. I was at the cinema with a very pretty girl who liked me. What more could I ask from life?

Joel already had his arm around Katie. I decided to make my move after the trailers. The first one was for a new horror spoof which looked promising. And then up on the screen I saw it: *blood*. Instantly my whole body just gave a massive lurch. I couldn't believe it. But suddenly blood was all I could think about.

I told myself not to be stupid. The blood on the screen wasn't even real – just tomato sauce or something. But it didn't matter. The need for blood pounded through me so strongly that I was actually sweating. And my heart was pounding away just as if I'd been running really fast in a race. Blood had to fill my mouth now. So I reached into my pocket for my little bottle of 'medicine'. I figured I only needed to drink a few drops and then this blood fever would pass. And provided I wiped my lips thoroughly with my hankie afterwards, Julie would never guess what I'd been doing.

So I started fumbling about for my bottle. Only it wasn't there. Then, with a stab of horror, I realized I must have left it in my school trousers. I'd been so busy styling my hair and covering myself in deodorant, I'd forgotten all about the 'medicine'. Now I was starting to panic. What could I do? Absolutely nothing; I'd just have to sit here until the end of the film and think about other things – like Julie.

She was so pretty and had a great personality and even laughed at my jokes and she— But it was no good. I couldn't shake off the blood fever which kept rising up into my throat. I bared my teeth in total frustration.

That's when Julie whispered, 'You can put your arm around me if you like.'

I wanted to do just that. Only not right now. So I hesitated.

'But only if you want to.' Now Julie sounded a bit offended and upset. The very last thing I wanted.

'Of course I want to,' I whispered. 'But it's such a big step, isn't it?' What was I babbling on about? I didn't know. I just knew my whole body was throbbing with my need for blood. I had to do something, anything to distract myself. 'Popcorn,' I shouted to Julie. 'Let's have some, shall we?' She looked just a tiny bit alarmed now. I smiled suavely at her, then I tried to open the box of popcorn in an easy-going, charming way. But that's impossible when your hands are shaking so much you can't even hold the box steady and you send half its contents flying onto the floor. Popcorn

111

scattered all around our feet and disturbed Joel and Katie.

'Hey, Marcus, what are you playing at?' groaned Joel.

'Sorry about that,' I said.

'Oh, it really doesn't matter,' said Julie. 'Anyway, there's still some left, isn't there?'

I tried to reply, but instead this funny little roar just escaped out of my mouth.

Julie giggled. 'You're in a crazy mood tonight, aren't you?'

She had no idea.

But I laughed and so did she.

'Actually, I'd heard you were a bit mad,' she went on, 'but I like boys like that.'

'You're going to like me a lot then,' I said. We were getting on so well. And she was brilliant, but I couldn't sit still because every second without blood was total agony. I'd have to leave her and ring Mum.

Mum said she'd rush over when I got a blood fever attack and she could probably get here in a few minutes. Then I'd meet her in the foyer, gulp down the blood and then race back to Julie and the others. It wasn't an ideal solution at all, but what else could I do?

So just as the main film was about to start I sprang up and whispered to Julie, 'I'm going to get us some more popcorn.'

'Oh, don't worry about that,' said Julie.

'No, it's not right to have only half a box. Why, you'll be through that before the credits. I'll be back before you know it,' I added optimistically.

Joel was staring at me too. 'Where are you going?'

'Popcorn,' I muttered, and then sped off.

The moment I reached the foyer I rang Mum. I said hoarsely, urgently, 'Mum, I'm still thirsty,' and then added, 'I forgot my medicine too.'

Mum let out a sharp breath and then cried, 'I shall move with all speed. So where are you?'

'Just inside the cinema.'

'Right.' And then she added, 'Are you very thirsty?'

'Never felt more thirsty! It's agony, Mum.'

'Don't worry,' she cried and hung up.

Then I noticed the woman in the box office watching me very curiously. 'You can't hang about here,' she called.

'I just need some medicine,' I explained, 'and then I'm going back into the film.' Then I let out another low but this time extremely fierce roar. Again, it just came out of nowhere. And the woman's mouth opened very wide as if she was going to scream. She didn't, but she never said another word either.

Now, hurry up, Mum.

9.00 p.m.

Still no sign of her, and now I need blood so much that I feel sick. I keep licking my lips, imagining the moment when it will trickle down my mouth.

9.06 p.m.

Then Joel appeared in the foyer, looking both confused and very angry (something Joel hardly ever is).

'Hey, what's going on?' he demanded. 'Why are you hanging about here? The film's started, you know, and Julie's really upset. She thinks you don't like her.'

'Of course I like her. It's just I . . . I feel a bit sick,' I said. 'But I'm fine, or I will be soon.

You go back; I'll join you in about two minutes.'

But Joel carried on staring at me and then he noticed a car pull up outside the cinema and someone rush out. He turned to me incredulously. 'Your mum's just arrived.'

'Has she?' I said as casually as I could.

'What's she doing here?'

'Come to see the film too, I expect.'

'Your mum's come here to see the film too? That's quite a coincidence.'

'Yes, it is, isn't it? Anyway, I really don't want you missing it.'

Joel moved closer to me. 'Marcus, are you slipping off home?'

'No.'

'Because I think that's a pretty mean thing to do to Julie.'

'I wouldn't do that, even if I didn't like Julie, but I do like her.'

'So why are you standing here waiting for your mum?'

'You remember a while back I was ill,' I said desperately. 'Well, that illness has come back. Not a lot – just a little bit – and one dollop of medicine should cure it and I'll be as

115

fit as a flea again. And here's Mum with it now,' I added, as she sped into the cinema.

'Hi, Mum,' I called. 'Got my medicine, have you?' And then once again to my utter amazement I let out this low but fierce growl. I didn't blame Joel at all for jumping back from me.

'Hello, Joel,' said Mum as brightly as she could. 'Just had an SOS from Marcus for his medicine.'

The woman in the box office called over to us. 'This is not a meeting place, you know.'

'Probably best if you take your medicine outside,' said Mum.

'Yeah, OK.'

I turned to Joel, who was watching all this with a look of utter bewilderment on his face.

'What exactly is wrong with you, mate?' he hissed.

'I've got a very low-grade virus,' I gibbered, 'which has extremely high-grade moments – like now. But once I go outside and take this medicine I'll be back to very low-grade. OK?' Before he could reply I said, 'You go and tell Julie I'll see her really soon.' And I suddenly remembered something I'd said to Gracie

116

about how weird people were the only ones worth knowing. Well, right now I'd give anything – *anything* – just to be a normal boy on a date.

9.08 p.m.

Outside the cinema I gulped down the entire contents of my 'medicine bottle'. At first the blood felt so hot I was afraid my teeth were going to melt. But Mum said this is quite normal during blood fever attacks. Normal! I don't know how she dared use the word.

My whole body tingled with delight and satisfaction. But it wasn't enough.

'You're still hungry, aren't you?' said Mum.

I nodded gloomily. 'You'll have to come home now, then,' said Mum.

'But what about Julie?' I said.

'You really can't go back to her right now,' said Mum softly.

So I scribbled a note to leave at the box office:

Dear Julie
My low-grade virus has flared up so I've got to leave to get treatment. Truly

sorry, as I think you're great. Hope you liked the film. I owe you a bag of popcorn!

Kindest regards,
Marcus

CHAPTER FIFTEEN

Saturday 10 November

9.05 a.m.

There must have been, in the history of the world, more disastrous dates than mine – but none comes readily to mind. And the truly maddening thing about it all is that Julie liked me and I liked her. And under normal circumstances . . . but I'm a half-vampire, which means I never know what's going on or what I'm turning into.

AND I HATE IT. REALLY, REALLY HATE IT!

11.45 a.m.

I rang Joel and tried to apologize. He just

119

snarled down the phone that Katie's so furious about how I messed Julie around that she's dumped him!

He added, 'And on no account are you to try and contact Julie. She doesn't ever want to hear your name again. Perhaps it's best if you go with your mum to the cinema in future.'

11.55 a.m.
My main ambition now is to crawl away under a stone and die quietly.

12.15 p.m.
Oh, but my mum tells me breezily not to be down-hearted. And last night was just a little blip. 'There'll be plenty more dates at the cinema,' she said.

'Oh yeah, they'll be queuing up to go out with me and I'll be ringing my mum to take me home before the main film starts.'

'This all seems very big and important now,' said Mum. 'But it'll be quickly forgotten. And we have got some good news for you.'

'Why is your good news always the total opposite?' I asked wearily.

Mum looked hurt for a moment, then said confidently, 'Well, this news will knock your socks off. Usually someone of your age wouldn't have a blood fever attack for weeks and weeks yet. Having it so early is highly unusual.'

'And that's the good news, is it? I'm even more highly unusual than I was before. Wow, Mum, you really know how to cheer someone up.'

'You didn't let me finish,' said Mum. 'Having a blood fever attack so early means you could have a special gift all of your own.'

'At this very moment,' chipped in Dad, 'a unique talent could be forming inside you.'

'So one day I'll find I can juggle or wiggle my ears . . .'

'Oh, something much more special than that,' said Mum.

'Maybe I'll be a wizard,' I said. 'I've always wanted to be one of those, as they wear such great hats.'

'We don't know what your special gifts will be,' said Dad. 'And, of course, it's not definitely confirmed until you have your second and last blood fever attack.'

'There's something not to look forward to,' I muttered.

'But afterwards it could be really exciting,' said Mum, and there was a sparkle in her eyes, which is hardly ever there when she's looking at me. 'So, Marcus, you really can aim for the stars,' she cooed.

You know what, blog, you can keep the stars, every last one of them.

1.15 p.m.

I'm not allowed to leave the house for the rest of the weekend either. 'It's very important you don't leave the house for a second,' said Dad.

Apparently, after a blood fever attack I need to be 'under observation' for forty-eight hours. Dad says this is because my behaviour is still highly unpredictable. It's probably just some stupid health and safety rule. But, of course, my parents have to make a big deal of everything and can never let me forget for a moment that I'm a half-vampire.

1.17 p.m.

I so want to talk to someone about all this.

But there's no one, until I suddenly realize: there is.

1.35 p.m.

I rang Gracie. Of course, I couldn't tell her exactly what happened with Julie last night – who knows who could be listening in? And a half-vampire's double life must be kept secret at all times. So we chatted in a kind of code.

'Hi, Flame,' I said.

She giggled. 'How are you doing, Ved?'

'I took a girl to the cinema last night,' I said.

'Oh yes.'

'Only I had to leave her after a few minutes because I felt very, very thirsty.'

It took Gracie a couple of seconds to work out what I was saying and then she gasped in horror and laughed. 'Sorry, it's not at all funny.'

I told her some more. She carried on gasping and laughing.

'I know, send her a text,' said Gracie. 'Tell her you had a stomach bug and didn't want to projectile vomit on her. That's why you left so quickly.'

'Apparently she doesn't even want to hear my name again.'

'She's taken it badly then.'

'So badly that Katie's dumped Joel and is spending all her time comforting Julie.'

'Oh, honestly,' cried Gracie, 'Julie's going right over the top now. I mean, you paid for her ticket and left her some popcorn. You just didn't stick around. I think humans totally overreact about everything. Imagine if they had our lives – but I'd better not say any more on the phone, had I?'

'No, just tell me how your hair's growing now.'

'Oh, I've got a lovely piece dangling off my chin now. I feel like the ugliest girl in the world today. I only have to walk past a mirror to shatter it. Still, hearing about your miserable love life has really cheered me up.'

'Oh good, well, if I have any other disasters . . .'

'Ring me right away,' she said.

7.20 p.m.

Just when I thought this weekend couldn't get any worse, I've now had a massive row with Tallulah. She rang up and didn't even bother saying hi or anything vaguely social like that. No, she just hissed, 'Have you got it?'

For a second I couldn't think what she was talking about.

'Got what?'

She sighed impatiently. 'The chain.'

'No, I haven't.'

'You haven't even been looking, have you?'

'Well, actually, I've been busy with more important stuff.'

'More important!' she echoed disbelievingly.

'Like on Friday night I went out on a date.' I didn't really know why I was bringing up that disaster. Yes, I do. I hoped somehow it might stir up a bit of jealousy in Tallulah. 'You might ask me how it went,' I said.

'Why, when I couldn't care less?'

Somehow, this comment really irritated me. So I snapped, 'But, of course, you never have time for anybody – except vampires, do you?'

'I just rang up to tell you something,' she

snapped back, 'though I don't know why I'm bothering now.'

'Do tell me please, because my life would be totally incomplete if you didn't give me the latest vampire news.'

'You're in a funny mood. I suppose Julie likes it when you say stupid things.'

'So you know who I went out with then.'

'Oh yeah, I know. But much more important: I'm one million per cent certain Giles is the vampire. He has to be. And even though a certain person has lost the chain, I'm going to stake out his house later tonight and follow him. I wouldn't be surprised if he led us to a whole nest of vampires.'

'Excuse me, but did you just say "us"?'

'Yes . . .' she began.

'So you don't even bother asking me? You just assume I'm going to spend Saturday night hanging outside some twerpy idiot's house, because you think he's a vampire?'

'A super-vampire, actually,' cried Tallulah.

'Well, you know what? I don't care, because I'm bored of hearing about vampires. I'm even more bored of trailing them—'

'May I just remind you of one fact?'

Tallulah interrupted. 'I didn't ask you to come with me to Mrs Lenchester's – you brought yourself along. Since then, all you've done is make stupid jokes and lose the most valuable thing we had – the chain. Actually, I don't know why I bothered ringing you, as I don't need you – *and I don't want you coming along*!'

That last line was shouted right in my ear. Then the phone crashed down.

She was extremely angry. I suppose I had been very forceful – stunned myself, actually. But I'd only told her the truth. The very last thing in the world I wanted to do tonight was hang about outside Giles's house. I mean, if he was a vampire – or super-vampire – and that was a massive if, why on earth should I want to get back on his radar? Especially as, if I annoyed him again, it might not just be bad dreams he sent me next time.

He could do anything.

No, let Tallulah rant and rave and sulk all she likes – I refuse to be sucked into this any more.

7.25 p.m.

Of course, there was an outside chance that Giles was . . . well, let's just say deeply dodgy. And Tallulah hadn't a clue what she was getting herself into. She didn't know the truth about vampires – as I did.

7.27 p.m.

So should I let her trail Giles on her own? What if something bad happened to her tonight?

7.28 p.m.

But I'm not staking out Giles's house all evening. I'm determined on that. I shall just nip along and see Tallulah and make her realize the danger she's putting herself in. After which, I'll come straight home. Of course, Tallulah will totally ignore my warning – but my conscience will be clear.

7.45 p.m.

I'd been wondering how I was going to get out past my parents. But in the end it was quite easy, as some neighbours called round raising money for something or other. And both Mum and Dad make a big point of belonging to the human community and supporting stuff. So when they were all yattering away at the front door, I sneaked out of the back one.

8.15 p.m.

I've just cut through Brent Woods. And it's a horrible night: cold, grey and starting to rain. But that's not what is bothering me. It's that I feel really strange. And I can't lose the feeling either. It's as if I'm not really myself tonight.

Don't ask me who I am. But I feel all mixed up and disorientated, like someone who's just been woken up in the middle of the night. I even said aloud to myself what my name was and where I lived.

And then something Dad said came rushing back: *It's very important you don't leave the house for a second.* I sort of understand what he means now. But I can't stop, can I?

I've got to go on.

CHAPTER SIXTEEN

Saturday 10 November

9.05 p.m.

I hovered outside Giles Wallace's house. No sign of Tallulah. So I started roaming about a bit. I passed the newsagent's shop. It was still open, and outside was a placard for the local paper: WILD BEAST STRIKES AGAIN. My stomach twisted about uneasily when I saw that. Then I felt angry. This whole vampire thing was like a huge black cloud which just followed me about wherever I turned, and there it was again.

It was all Tallulah's fault, pulling me into all this. I started walking about some more. It was raining quite hard now and I could hear the drops pattering down on all the cars in the road. Then I heard another sound. A great hacking cough which just erupted out of the bus shelter. And there was Tallulah, reading the local paper.

'You sound healthy,' I said.

'Go away,' she cried.

I really wanted to do just that, but instead I said, 'Hey, this is a bus shelter, anyone can wait here – even me. And go on, admit it, aren't you secretly pleased I've come to keep you company?'

'No,' she hissed, 'because you'll ruin everything.'

'Why, what's happened?'

'Nothing to do with you.' She turned round and scowled at me. She was deathly pale and looked as if she'd been awake for a hundred years. She obviously still wasn't over her flu.

'I'm amazed your parents let you out tonight,' I said.

'They don't know anything about it. But there's a super-vampire on the loose and it's up to me to do something about it' – she patted the newspaper fiercely – 'and fast.' Then she added excitedly, 'Giles has gone in there.' She pointed at the house directly opposite the bus shelter. 'And now he's coming out again.'

'A life packed with excitement,' I said, leaning against the bus shelter. My head was really spinning now and I had this horrible tight feeling in my stomach, just as if I was about to be extremely sick.

'Giles is coming down the drive,' said Tallulah, and started to cough again. Both of us, I thought, should be tucked up at home now, not out here on some wild-goose chase. I was about to say this to Tallulah, but instead, something quite different happened.

My stomach grew even tighter and I let out a deep, menacing growl. It came from right at the back of my throat and it was pretty loud.

Tallulah gaped at me. 'What are you doing?'

I struggled to answer, but instead another even fiercer growl pushed its way out of my mouth. And it had absolutely nothing to do with me. It was a bit like when you get the hiccups – they just escape, don't they, you can't control them. The trouble was, my sound effects were much louder and weirder than hiccups.

It was no surprise that Giles suddenly popped his head round the side of the shelter. He was wearing a hat tonight, with the brim pulled right down, making him look more mysterious. He also had a small briefcase under his arm. His voice was as fake-chummy as ever, though.

'My goodness,' he said to me, 'we meet again. Do you know, I thought we had an animal escaped from the zoo out here.'

I grinned awkwardly. 'I've just been trying to impress my girlfriend with a few of my animal noises,' I said.

'Only I'm not his girlfriend,' added Tallulah promptly.

Giles gave a fat, smug smile. 'And where are you both off to – somewhere interesting?'

'No,' began Tallulah, 'we're not going any-where. Well, I mean, we are, but not together.' She began to cough again.

Giles pulled a concerned face. 'My good-ness, that cough doesn't sound very healthy. Well, I'm off home but I'm absolutely certain our paths will cross again.' Was there a hint of menace in his voice as he said this? 'And congratulations on those animal noises. I was impressed, even if your girlfriend wasn't.'

Then he was gone. And Tallulah turned on me, eyes blazing. 'You know you've sabotaged tonight's mission, don't you? There's no way I can follow him now.'

'He said he's just going home.'

'Well, he is now,' she cried, 'since he knows we're on to him. But what was the point of all those pathetic noises? I mean, it was vital we stayed undercover tonight. You've ruined everything.' She was practically crying with frustration.

And I felt bad as every word she'd said was true. 'I'm really sorry, Tallulah, but I'm just not myself tonight.'

'Actually, what you did was pathetically typical of you. You think you're so funny, don't you? Well, you're not, you're just a big pain.'

She left the bus shelter and walked quickly away. 'Where are you going?' I asked.

'As far away from you as possible.'

I tried to say something else, but instead, another animal cry – this time a wild, trumpeting elephant-on-the-rampage kind of noise – just burst out of my mouth.

Tallulah whirled round, shot me a look of total contempt and then sped away. Meanwhile, a woman across the road was gaping at me, open-mouthed with shock. 'Toothache,' I yelled over to her. 'I've got this really bad toothache.' After which I let off another mad animal noise and the woman just fled up that road.

What was happening to me?

I just knew I had to go home *now*.

9.58 p.m.

I pelted back through Brent Woods. Even before all these recent attacks, it really was not a place to linger in, especially as it had got dark so fast. The darkness was as thick as marmalade too, and as sticky. It seemed to have smeared itself over everything. So I wasn't even sure if I was running in the right direction. It wasn't an especially big wood, and it was a real short cut. But tonight I wished I'd taken the long way round as I managed to get completely lost.

It was so quiet too. In fact, the silence was

louder than someone shouting. No birds were rustling about tonight. They must have all had an early night. And even the rain seemed to have been fitted with silencers. The only noise was the thump of my footsteps on the damp dead leaves as I tore wildly towards what I hoped was the end of this wood.

But all the time I had an uneasy feeling I was being watched by someone who was keeping deathly still, just waiting for the right moment to pounce. Perhaps Giles . . . ? No, total rubbish. Giles was at home now. These woods were creeping me out, that's all.

And then, quite suddenly, I came skidding to a halt. For I had heard something.

It was a cry. A cry of total terror.

Tallulah. That was my first thought and my second. She'd gone speeding through the woods, but had fallen over and now was in great pain. But the cry had sounded so high and kind of eerie I wondered if it was human at all. Could it be an animal caught in a trap? But then I decided it had to be a human. And it was coming from somewhere on the ground near me.

I crouched down, trying somehow to peer

through the darkness. 'Hey there!' I called. 'I want to help you, so just call out or grunt or burp. Anything, so I know where you are. Come on, don't be shy.'

I listened hard: silence, except for the rain, which suddenly started swishing down really heavily. I knelt even lower. 'Hey, I know you're out there and I really do want to help you.'

And the next moment I did hear something. A flap of a wing just above my head. There in front of me was a huge bat, about the size of a seagull. And it was hurtling itself right at me. Any second now its teeth would sink into my neck. After which I'd pass out almost immediately, and then it would move in for my blood. I knew all this because it had happened to me once before in these very woods.

And it was about to happen again.

From out of nowhere this bat plunged right at my face, sending me sprawling backwards and knocking all the breath out of my body. But I couldn't let myself be attacked again. I had to fight back this time.

So I hit out wildly as the bat launched

itself at my neck. 'Sorry, but blood's off the menu tonight,' I gasped. Then another of those strange animal cries jumped out of my mouth. But it didn't bother the bat at all.

Instead it started dive-bombing me at a ferocious speed.

But a new energy suddenly seemed to pulse right through me. I was like Popeye after he'd had a double helping of spinach.

And that was really so strange, because normally I'm as rubbish at fighting as I am at running. But tonight I was beating away at that giant bat with incredible speed and determination. Nothing could put me off. Not even when, with a great scream of rage, it flew at my eyes. I just carried on roaring and punching.

Until, just as suddenly as it had appeared, it vanished.

I leaned over, catching my breath, utterly exhausted. But out of the corner of my eye, I saw something stirring, or I thought I did. Was it the bat returning for Round Two? Or was my imagination in over-drive?

I wasn't sure.

I just knew I had to get out of the woods as

quickly as I could. But I was shattered now, hardly able to put one foot in front of the other. And I still wasn't exactly sure where I was going.

That's when I had an idea: to transform into a bat myself. That way I could fly right up into the sky and get a much better view of where I was. I could fly much quicker than I could walk too.

But I'd only been able to transform once. All my later efforts had been dismal failures. But something told me it was worth a go. So tonight I started walking about on tiptoe – I always feel really silly doing this bit – and then desperately tried to empty my mind and think about absolutely nothing. Funny how I can do that so easily in double maths.

And suddenly, amazingly, I was able to do it now too. Almost before I knew it, I'd whooshed right up into the air as a bat. I almost wished my parents could see this speedy transformation. They'd be stunned.

Then I remembered my dad's advice: *the moment you transform, always point your face up at the sky*. I could see exactly where I was too. Why, I was practically at the end of the woods. It shouldn't take me long to fly out of here, provided I didn't crash into something.

But what about that person – or animal – who'd yelled out? I started to fly about, just to check no one was lying there in total agony. I couldn't see anyone.

And then I could.

The unmistakable figure of Giles Wallace. Now in human form, and holding a torch.

He seemed to be searching for someone. *Me!* He obviously had no idea I could transform and was getting ready for Round Two. So Tallulah was right: he really *was* the vampire.

I soared right above him. Being a bat is just so cool, you know. It is a bit like you've transformed into a superhero, as I could fly at such an incredible speed. Before I knew it I'd reached my road. It was deserted except for one figure half running and looking very anxious – my dad. He was speaking into his mobile. 'There's no sign of him anywhere. If you start ringing around his friends, I'll—'

Then a bat dived down out of a pitch-dark

sky and whispered in his ear, 'Hi, Dad, this rain's a pain, isn't it?'

Dad jumped in the air as if he were about to start performing some big dance routine. 'Marcus . . . is that you?'

'The very same.'

'I've just been out looking everywhere for you,' he whispered grumpily. 'You gave your mum and me such a scare just going out like that, especially as we expressly told you . . . so where have you been?'

'Oh, just out,' I said casually. 'Then it started to rain so I flew home.'

'And how long have you been transformed.'

'Oh, ages and ages,' I said. 'Nearly fifteen minutes, at least.'

Dad couldn't help a proud smile escaping across his face now, and then he whispered, 'Fly round to the back, will you?'

'But why?'

'Well, seeing you airborne is such a great moment,' he said, 'I want to take some pictures.'

CHAPTER SEVENTEEN

Saturday 10 November

10.45 p.m.

Mum and Dad sent for Dr Jasper – the half-vampires' own special doctor – to give me a quick check-up. He's a small gnome-like man who peered at me with a mixture of concern and amusement through a huge magnifying glass.

'Going out alone when you had a blood fever attack only the night before.' He shook his head. 'You like to make life difficult for yourself, don't you? Still, no harm done this time. You've been lucky. I suppose you were sneaking out to see a girl.'

'See that with your magnifying glass too,

did you, Doc?' I grinned. I went on to tell him, and Mum and Dad, a bit of the truth – namely how I met a girl at a bus stop and then, in the middle of our conversation, I started doing animal noises. 'I couldn't stop doing them, in fact.'

'And what did the girl say?' asked Dr Jasper.

'Well, she wasn't very impressed. In fact, she stalked off.'

'Oh dear, poor Marcus,' said Mum. 'You're not having much luck with your young ladies lately, are you?' And she started telling Dr Jasper about my date at the cinema. Soon all three were convulsed with laughter.

'Well, I'm glad my miserable love life is causing such merriment,' I said.

This only made them laugh even louder. 'Oh, it's not funny,' said Mum, wiping her eyes.

'Well, when you've all calmed down, answer this,' I said. 'Why did I suddenly make all those weird noises at the bus stop anyway?'

Dr Jasper explained, 'Most of the time your vampire side dozes quietly, only showing itself in little gifts like being able to fly. But during a blood fever attack your vampire nature wakes up and is just raging to be let out. And at moments of stress or anxiety it can't be held back.'

'And when I suddenly found I could fly home?' I asked.

'You've always been able to do that,' said the doctor, 'but your human side put up barriers and stopped you. During blood fever, though, your vampire nature smashes through and shows what you really can do. You might also find you have a special skill immediately after a blood fever attack, like being able to read minds or send messages to someone close to you or becoming suddenly immensely strong.'

So that's how I was able to fight Giles in the woods.

'But tomorrow the blood fever attack will be over and you'll be back to normal,' said Dr Jasper.

And do you know, for a moment there I was disappointed. I'd really liked having all that extra strength. 'But there will be another blood fever attack?' I asked. And I couldn't keep the eagerness out of my voice. Mum and Dad noticed this and smiled in a highly pleased way at each other.

'A second and last blood fever attack will certainly roll up,' said Dr Jasper.

'When?' I asked.

'It might not be for weeks and weeks yet,' said Dad. 'Or it could happen very soon indeed.'

'And if it happens again very soon,' I said, 'does that mean I've got this special gift Mum and Dad have been gibbering about?'

'There is absolutely no guarantee you will have your next attack soon,' said Dr Jasper firmly. 'But I will say just this, Marcus. If by some amazing chance you have your second blood fever attack soon – well then, it could be the start of the greatest possible adventure of your life.' He got up. 'Now, not another word about it from any of you – and that's doctor's orders.'

Sunday 11 November

12.15 a.m.
The greatest possible adventure of your life.

Dr Jasper's words are still ringing in my ears. Perhaps that's why I'm not scared of Giles tonight. I defeated him once in the woods, and I'm sure I can beat him again. So send me a nightmare, Giles, or get me sleep-walking. Or better still, turn up yourself for Round Two. Yeah, I'll fight you again. I don't care. *Just bring it on!*

11.30 a.m.
Can you believe it, I've only just woken up. Straight after a blood fever attack is the one time half-vampires need lots of extra sleep apparently. My throat is feeling really dry too. But that's a sign it's over.

11.45 a.m.
Last night I'd been so thrilled about being a half-vampire and that blood fever attack. But this morning I can't find that part of myself anywhere. It's as if I was put under a spell yesterday which has now well and truly worn off.

3.15 p.m.
I've just rung Tallulah.

'Hi, I just wanted to check you got home all right yesterday.'

'And why shouldn't I?'

'Well, I got set upon by a vampire on the way back, that's why.' But I don't say this. Instead, I asked: 'And how are you feeling?'

'Better when you ring off.'

'Hey, don't be like that, but look, I can see why you're a bit cross. I'm so sorry for those ani—'

'I still can't work out why you did it,' she interrupted. 'I mean, at first I wondered if you were paying me back for not going to the cinema with you.'

'Hey, that was your decision. The wrong one, but I'd never be so petty—'

'Then,' she swept on, 'I decided you thought you were protecting me and keeping me out of danger. That's why you pretended to lose Mrs Lenchester's chain.'

'I didn't pretend; I really did lose it.'

'The other alternative, however, is . . . that you're just an idiot.'

'Now you're getting warm.'

'Anyway, I don't care why you did it, but I shall carry on alone.'

'Oh now, hold on.'

'No, you're off this mission.'

Actually, I'd love to be off this mission, but somehow I just couldn't bring myself to abandon Tallulah, especially now I'd discovered that Giles is almost certainly a super-vampire.

'You'll let me help a bit, though,' I said coaxingly.

'No!'

'Well, we can still be friends.'

Her voice sounded a bit more muffled now. 'I'm sorry, I don't really do friends. And you're . . .' She paused.

'Yes?' I prompted.

'You're not what I thought you were.' Somehow those words hit me just as if I'd been punched.

And before I could reply she'd rung off.

9.05 p.m.

The only good thing about today has been all the texts I've had from Gracie. We've taken to calling each other by our half-vampire names. My parents and her mum definitely wouldn't approve – half-vampire names are supposed to be kept completely secret from humans. So they certainly shouldn't be trusted to texts.

And, of course, Gracie and I are just using these names as a joke, which would have infuriated my parents. So it's a joke which actually only Gracie and I can share. It's strange how close you can feel to someone you've only met three days ago. I even wanted to tell her about Giles Wallace, but I couldn't place all that on her.

9.50 p.m.

I'm certain it was Giles who attacked me in Brent Woods last night. Well, I actually saw him there just after I'd been attacked. And that couldn't be another coincidence. He probably sent me those nightmares too, and got me to throw the chain down to him.

So now it's time to tell someone else that he is a vampire. But who?

Here are my nominees:

First of all, Tallulah. She'd be excited to have her belief that Giles is a vampire confirmed and really eager to take him on. But what could she do against a vampire –

149

especially a super-vampire? Plus, the very last thing I'd want is for her to be the victim of a Giles attack.

Next, my dad. But vampires are Premier League creatures, while half-vampires would be lucky to make Division Three. Dad would be no match for Giles.

Besides, if I did tell him, I'd never hear the end of it. Aren't he and Mum always telling me to stay away from vampires?

That leaves only one option: Elsa Lenchester. I didn't look forward at all to telling her that I'd lost the chain, but I'd even do that just so I could hand over the case to someone else. And really, she's the ideal person. After all, she's the one who put us on to the local vampire in the first place, so she's bound to know what to do next.

I'll go and see her tomorrow.

CHAPTER EIGHTEEN

Monday 12 November

8.15 a.m.

'Highly unlikely you'll get another craving yet,' said Mum, 'but this is just in case it should happen again really quickly,' and she gave an excited little gasp as she handed me a fresh bottle of blood.

I pretended to look really keen too.

9.05 a.m.

I ventured into school more than a bit cautiously. I was on the look-out for people – and girls especially – to erupt into loud derisive laughter as soon as I was sighted. For if the news about my antics at the cinema on Friday had got out, well, I'd be the joke of the school. And days and days of social humiliation awaited me.

A gang of girls were hanging about in the playground. Some of them are in my year and good friends with Julie. But they ignored me, as usual. So far so good.

Next I spotted Joel. He saw me and then looked all around.

'So where is she?'

'Who?' I asked.

'Your mummy, or is it only on dates that she comes too?'

'Wow, you're such a funny guy,' I began. 'But I was very ill.'

'Well, you're bursting with health now.'

'Yeah, it was one of those twenty-four-hour low-grade maximum-misery bugs which come and go really fast. You must have heard of them,' I added hopefully. 'They're really quite famous.'

Joel didn't say anything for a moment. Then he laughed, but it was a cold, dead laugh. And he muttered, 'You're such a liar.'

I tried to change the subject. 'I don't suppose you know how Julie is?' I asked.

'I know she never wants to hear your name again, unless it's to say you've left on a doomed mission to Mars.'

'How about you and Katie—?'

'We're still history,' he snapped. Then he added unexpectedly, 'Katie won't say anything about Friday to anyone else, though.'

I was so grateful and surprised I didn't know what to say. So I just did my impression of a deeply shocked goldfish while Joel went on.

'She's keeping quiet – not for your sake or mine, but because Julie knows a lot of people at our school and Julie would hate them to find out how she was humiliated.'

'Well, it's a relief anyway,' I said. 'Not a relief that Julie thinks she was humiliated, of course, but that she won't tell anyone.' I was gabbling, but Joel was making me uneasy. It was the odd way he kept looking at me, as if I'd suddenly turned into someone he didn't really know or like very much.

'You know, I really do hope you and Katie get back together,' I said. 'And if I can do anything to help—'

'Don't you bother,' interrupted Joel, 'and

there's about as much chance of me and Katie going out again as there is of Julie going on another date with you.'

Julie and I probably are a lost cause, but Joel and Katie were a totally different matter. And despite what Joel said, I was going to do something about that.

11.00 a.m.
Tallulah was away again today. I was relieved, as it meant I could slip off to Elsa's house after school on my own. But also just a little bit concerned – Tallulah seemed to be having a lot of days off recently.

4.05 p.m.
I'd just reached Elsa's house when my mobile went off. It was my mum checking everything was all right. She sounded a bit disappointed when I said I hadn't even had the glimmer of a blood fever attack.

5.15 p.m.
I rapped on the door with the knocker. And then, through the frosted glass, I saw Elsa slowly, jerkily hobbling towards the door. She

seemed especially frail today. What could she possibly do against Giles? But she must have other contacts. And it was up to them to take over now.

She opened the door with a cat in her arms – the deadly Rufus. He hissed as soon as he saw me. 'Naughty Rufus,' she said, 'but you must remember this young man.'

'Hi there, Elsa, I'll certainly never forget him,' I said.

'And where's your friend today?' she asked.

'She's not well.'

'Oh dear, but you're the boy with the power, aren't you?'

'Yeah, that's me all right ... actually, I've got quite a lot to tell you.'

She undid all the chains on the door. There were about ninety of them, but she said she was taking extra precautions because the couple who live in the cottage next door to her had gone away for a while. 'And I'm so isolated here,' she said a bit sadly. Then she added, 'Would you believe, the kettle has just boiled? So I must have sensed you were coming.'

Or maybe you just drink a lot of tea, I

thought. A few minutes later Elsa and I were sitting in her musty old room with a large tray of tea and home-made biscuits. But it felt odd without Tallulah here too. She belonged in this. But it also meant I could chat more freely about what had happened.

And I did. I told Elsa about everything that had occurred, even the strange nightmares. It was kind of a relief to do that too. I felt as if I was off-loading everything onto poor old Elsa (although, as I kept reminding myself, she did get me into all this in the first place).

She sat listening so intently she even forgot to pick up her cup of tea. When I told her about losing the chain, I expected a sharp intake of breath at least. But she stayed remarkably calm and just said quietly, 'You didn't lose it. It was stolen from you.'

'By Giles?'

She considered for a moment. 'Everything seems to point to him,' she said slowly.

'So you really think he sent me that night-mare and—'

'Without a shadow of a doubt,' she interrupted. 'He couldn't leave you running

156

about with that chain. He'd already engaged you in conversation and picked up your worst fear. Vampires are such clever, intuitive people. Right from the start I'm sure he suspected you. He might even have walked into that shop deliberately that day just to find out what you were up to. Still' – she gave a deep chuckle – 'we've tracked him down. We've got him. If only my husband Fergus could be here to see this day, because the research was all his really. But now you – you clever boy – have proved my husband right. Well done, Marcus.'

I couldn't help beaming a bit. 'So what happens now, Elsa? Do we tell the police or the prime minister or the circus, or all three?'

'We can never tell anyone,' she said firmly. 'Most humans' minds are totally closed on this subject. And they have no idea of this other world, lying so very close to their own. No, this must remain our secret.'

I nodded, thinking the whole thing had been a bit pointless then.

'Normally, I would say to you that you've done very well locating the vampire,' she said. 'And it's too dangerous to go any

157

further. But I believe you can confront the vampire. Because you have the power.'

'Got your word on that, have I?'

'You're special. I saw that the moment you first appeared here.' Then she smiled. 'It seems a huge task, doesn't it, all on your own?'

'Yeah, I must admit I was hoping for more of a team effort.'

'But all you've got to do is take something that belongs to Giles Wallace.'

I grinned. 'How about his car?'

She grinned too. 'It could be something as simple as an old handkerchief.'

'Or maybe even something he puts out for recycling, like an old newspaper?' I suggest, thinking I could probably take that quite easily.

'No, it needs to be more personal than that. It can be very small. The important thing is that it has a vampire's smell on it. That's why an article of clothing is the best. If you take a vampire's belongings, it instantly weakens their power.'

'And what do I do with it after I've got it?' I asked.

'Just let him know you have it.'

'Oh, I see,' I said, although I didn't.

'My husband said there's a strongly-held belief amongst vampires that whoever takes something personal from them also gains a power over them. But only while that person keeps the object, so he will try his hardest to get it back from you. That's why you must immediately bring it here. I will hide it for you and see if we can force him into the open. If he feels humiliated, then we've got him for sure.'

At the door she said to me, 'I wish I could shake up these tired old bones and help you. But I'll be thinking about you. We all will,' she added, nodding at her cats, who had gathered around as if to see me off. Then she took my hand and whispered, 'This vampire must be stopped before he does any more harm and I know you're the person to do that.'

5.50 p.m.

Elsa stood at the door, waving me off until I was out of sight. I hate thinking about that now and the bright hopefulness in her eyes as she said, 'I know you're the person to do that.'

You see, I've got no intention of stealing anything from Giles – or, in fact, going anywhere near him again.

Yes, I beat Giles in that fight in the woods on Saturday night. But it was just lucky I was in the middle of a blood fever attack. In a way, it wasn't really me who took on Giles that night. But now, just thinking about another encounter with Giles makes me feel very, very tired – the sort of tiredness I feel at the start of term when I think of all those maths lessons looming over me.

And it's not just because maths is boring (although it definitely is); it's because I'm total rubbish at it. I'm total rubbish at being brave too, especially when I'm up against a single vampire. So that's why I've resigned from the operation.

I am sorry about Elsa, though. A tear even sneaked its way out of my eye when I thought of her waiting for me to come back. I'd have really liked to have seen her again and helped her out. But she'd want to know what I'd done about Giles, and when I told her nothing . . . well, she'd just be devastated.

So I'll never see Elsa again.

Or Giles either.

And not even Tallulah can change my mind this time.

CHAPTER NINETEEN

Monday 12 November

7.30 p.m.

I've just done something which made me cringe at lot. But I had no choice.

First off, as soon as I got home from Elsa's, I rang Katie.

'What do you want?' She was so distant she was hardly there.

I swallowed hard and said, 'I haven't told Joel what really happened on Saturday night, but I'll tell you now. On one condition: you don't say anything to him. You've got to promise.'

She was dead interested in what I had to say now all right. 'OK, I promise,' she said quickly.

I so hated what I had to say next. But if you want someone to believe you, it's got to be really humiliating. 'At the cinema on Friday,' I said, 'I got the runs. That's why I had to race to the loo, but it still wouldn't stop, if you know what I mean, and I think you do. So in the end I rang my mum to, er, take me away.'

'You still should have told Julie,' she said.

'You reckon?' I cried. 'So what do you suggest I say: "Hi, Julie, I've just popped back to tell you I've got the runs and totally stink right now"? Yeah, that's dead romantic, isn't it?'

I waited for a reaction from Katie, but instead this silence just stretched on. I even wondered if she'd rung off until I heard these smothered giggles.

'Hey, you're not laughing at me, are you?' I asked.

'No, no,' she spluttered.

'And you won't tell Joel, will you?'

'Oh no,' she said, not at all convincingly. 'Bye then, Marcus.'

I knew as soon as I put the phone down she was just going to laugh and laugh and then . . . Well, if me having the runs doesn't get

Joel and her talking again, I don't know what will.

I've been getting texts all day from Gracie. I guess she must get really bored stuck in that house on her own all the time. But now I got one saying:

Ved, ring me as soon as you can.

And when I did she practically yelled, 'The Bearded Woman is no more, because all her beard has just vanished.'

'Hey, that's excellent news.'

'I know . . . and even though it's not my birthday, Mum's baking a special cake tomorrow to celebrate. By the way, what's your opinion of birthday cake?'

'I'm a massive fan of it.'

'So, you're invited then,' she said a little breathlessly.

'Well, if I can get my parents to give me a lift – and I'm sure I can – I'll be there, for say about five o'clock.'

164

9.15 p.m.

'Of course we will give you a lift to Gracie's,' said Mum. 'And after tea, if you two want to chill out together – I believe that's the current expression, isn't it?' – she laughed delightedly at her imagined coolness – 'well, that's fine too, as your school's got an Inset day on Wednesday, hasn't it?'

'Of course it has,' I muttered. How could I have forgotten brilliant news like that?

'So you two can have a proper evening together, can't you,' continued Mum, who was in grave danger of turning into some kind of demented matchmaker. She was so keen she was putting me off, until I reminded myself that I really did like Gracie. In fact, I'd never met a girl I'd got on with better.

11.15 p.m.

Just as I was getting ready to go flitting in the back garden tonight, Dad said to me, 'You saw what you could do when you had a blood fever attack, so do the same now. Let the human side of yourself slip away and just enjoy being a half-vampire.'

And among all the acres of advice I've

received from Mum and Dad, this actually worked.

So tonight, while I was outside prancing about on tiptoe, I thought: *Ha, ha, ha, ha, ha, ha, I'm a happy half-vampire*, or something like that, and right away I felt this tingle shoot right down my body. And the next thing I knew I was up in the air and stayed there for six whole minutes, and just felt totally brilliant.

Afterwards my parents said I was 'a natural', which isn't true at all, but still, it was great to be flitting again.

Tuesday 13 November

7.25 a.m.

Just woken up from a deeply relaxing, uninterrupted four-hour sleep. And no spiders dropped down onto my face, and no sleepwalking that I can remember – just a perfectly ordinary (and that's not a word you see very often in this blog, is it?) night.

166

8.15 a.m.

On the local radio station they've been discussing these attacks in Brent Woods. They're still speculating on what kind of animal it could be. The latest is that it's some kind of giant wild cat, like a pole cat. Then I noticed Dad listening to the radio too. 'Stay right away from Brent Woods,' he said. Did he know what the creature really was? Hard to tell. But he was looking at me really fiercely.

So I just nodded in agreement.

9.03 a.m.

Joel was waiting at the school gate for me. I quickly discovered why.

'Katie rang me late last night,' he said.

'That's good,' I began.

'And she's undumped me. Is undumped a proper word? Don't know, don't care, but anyway, we're back together again.' He was talking so animatedly and I'm really pleased for him, even if I couldn't help a touch of jealousy sneaking in there too. It must be pretty decent having a girlfriend.

But I just said, 'You shouldn't have to

suffer for your mate's bad behaviour at the cinema.'

And straight away a giveaway twinkle appeared in Joel's eyes. Oh yes, Katie had told him about the runs all right. Then he patted me on the back and we walked into school together, just like we normally did. But I'd lost Joel there for a couple of days. And it was a big relief that we were mates again.

10.45 a.m.
Tallulah's still away. Is she still ill – or just skiving?

5.25 p.m.
I'm at Gracie's house, but no sign of that birthday cake yet – or in fact Gracie. Apparently, she's upstairs with a bad headache.

'I hope she'll be down soon,' said her mum. And her face couldn't look any redder. 'But when you've got a migraine you've just got to sit quietly, haven't you?'

'That's very, very true,' I said, while the minutes tottered on.

6.05 p.m.

Gracie finally appeared. And I could tell right away she'd been crying. 'Sorry about that,' she said to me, and then exclaimed, 'Oh, you haven't given Marcus any cake, Mum!'

'I thought we'd wait for you, dear,' said her mum. 'I was telling Marcus about your headache. It's better now, isn't it?'

'Oh, yeah,' she said vaguely. Her mum left to get the cake and Gracie said, 'I bet you think I'm a right moody cow, don't you, inviting you round and then not even being here? I mean, how rude is that?'

'I might be going out on a limb here – but I'm guessing you don't really have a headache.'

'Oh no, Mum just made that up. I was upset about something. Very upset.'

'So tell Uncle Ved all.'

'Well, you know my hair has gone.'

'I did sort of notice, yeah.'

'And now my life starts again, I thought. And then Mrs Walter from my school sent a text saying I could still audition to be in the school play. She's really keen for me to be in it, actually.'

'So you must be good,' I said.

Gracie smiled modestly and said, 'I was so happy until Mum sent a reply saying I was still too ill to even consider it.'

'Why did she do that?'

'Because I'll only have a few days of being normal, then it's back to being Beardie. Only next time even *more* hair will be sprouting all over me. And after Mum dropped *that* bombshell, she just said to me, "Are you OK, my dear?"'

And Gracie did such a brilliant impression of her mother saying that, I felt like applauding.

She went on, 'Mum doesn't understand. That's my big ambition – to be an actress.'

'And you still could be,' I say.

'Oh yeah, in horror movies. The girl who's so scary she doesn't need any make-up.'

'What's happening to you now is just a phase,' I say. 'You've got to keep reminding yourself about that. It does mess up your life big-time, though. And it must be really crushing when you miss out on the chance of being in a play—'

'Or getting a girlfriend,' she interrupted,

looking right at me suddenly.

'Oh, I've practically forgotten about that,' I replied. Then swiftly changing the subject, I said, 'So have they had you practising your howl yet?'

'My mum was on at me last night about that. Can you howl?'

'Can I howl?' I said. 'Just listen to this.' I put my head back and then released an ear-splitting, truly piercing howl, which even made the ornaments on the mantelpiece jump about.

'But that's incredible,' she cried.

'I know,' I agreed.

'You'll have to teach me.'

'Sure, of course.'

And then Gracie's mum came in. 'What a wonderful sound,' she said. 'Just give me a little bit of warning next time so I can make sure all the windows are closed.'

'Oh, sorry,' I said.

'No, not at all. We've just got one very nosy neighbour.' She was carrying Gracie's birth-day cake – but she couldn't stay long as she had to get herself ready to meet Gracie's new tutor.

'I can't even get out of doing lessons,' groaned Gracie.

'Well, we don't want you to fall too badly behind,' said her mum, 'and it's just for a little while. Someone to work with you intensively while you're—'

'Non-hairy,' interrupted Gracie.

'He's coming round shortly to discuss a few things with me. I just need you, Gracie, to come in and say hello, that's all. It will only be for a week or so – as soon as you have your next hairy attack, we'll cancel him; and after you've gone right through this phase, well, you can go back to school as normal. Won't that be nice?'

After her mum had left, Gracie said, 'How old do you think my tutor will be? A hundred and ten.'

'More like a hundred and twenty,' I said.

A car pulled up. 'I bet that's him,' said Gracie. She dashed to the window. 'Yeah, only he's not quite as old as I thought. Look!'

I got up to have a quick glance.

And I recognized the tutor instantly.

It was Giles Wallace.

CHAPTER TWENTY

Tuesday 13 November

6.45 p.m.

Vampires really like to be invited into a house, especially if it contains a half-vampire who hasn't yet changed over. Somehow in their warped minds this little bit of etiquette then gives them permission to drink their blood whenever they feel like it.

And Gracie was a half-vampire just like that. So her blood would be especially delicious to Giles. She was his target for certain. And with just Gracie and her mum in the house, he could strike very easily.

So I had to stop him coming in, didn't I? But then I could hear Gracie's mum talking to him. He'd already crossed the threshold and smelled the delicious scent of a half-vampire who hasn't yet transformed. And now he's gone into the dining room with Gracie's mum.

6.46 p.m.

Should I burst in on him? Order him out of the house right away? Yet how could I explain my reasons? And I'd probably terrify Gracie and her mum half to death. Then Gracie's mum would ring my parents. And they'd hit the roof if they heard I'd been trailing vampires.

But I couldn't just hang about. I had to do something. Gracie was in tremendous danger.

Meanwhile, Gracie was staring at me. 'What's the matter?'

'You won't believe this,' I said, 'but I recognize your tutor.' I began to talk really fast. 'A couple of my mates went to him for extra lessons – and the thing is, he's total rubbish. He didn't even teach them from the right syllabus. And they failed every one of their exams. They only got about four per cent. In fact, they reckon they'd have got higher marks if they'd not had any lessons from him at all. He put them totally and completely wrong.'

'Wow,' said Gracie. 'He sounds like the worst tutor in the whole world, but Mum said he had glowing references.'

'Which he wrote himself,' I said.

'No.'

'I wouldn't put anything past him.'

And then I heard Gracie's mum calling for her. 'I'd better go and say hello,' she said, 'even though Mum will probably cancel him afterwards.'

'OK, but be careful.'

Gracie whirled round. 'What do you mean by that?'

'Just, you know, don't be fooled by him and keep your wits about you.'

Gracie giggled. 'You really don't like him, do you?'

I shook my head. 'The stuff I've heard about him – you wouldn't believe it.'

6.55 p.m.
Gracie left, and I was just pacing about like a

caged animal. Blog, you've got to help me think calmly, logically.

I'm sure Giles wouldn't strike yet. No, he'll pick his moment. That could be soon, though. Best thing I can do now is to eavesdrop on what he is saying.

7.10 p.m.

But I only got as far as the hall. For there, hanging up, was Giles's huge black coat. And something Elsa said came rushing back:

If you take a vampire's belongings it instantly weakens their power.

When Elsa told me this yesterday, I was determined not to do anything. I really didn't want to get involved. I still don't. But I had no choice now, because if he did anything to Gracie . . .

His coat would be perfect. That would have his smell on it, all right. But could I just nick his coat? For a start he'd realize at once it was gone. There must be something inside his coat — like a handkerchief (Elsa had said that would be enough), or those gloves he strutted about in.

I took the coat off the peg and examined it.

Would you believe, right at the top were his initials: GW. What a poser. Still, I suppose vampires were the ultimate posers, swishing about in their cloaks (not to mention half-vampires – I've still got my cloak in my bedroom wardrobe). And really, this big coat was like Giles's cloak.

Then I quickly went through the coat pockets. Nothing. No hankie, no gloves. Not even a pen. All the pockets were empty. I couldn't believe it. And then I noticed, just inside the coat, was its label: *Modina*. That would have Giles's smell on it. That would count, wouldn't it?

I looked around for some scissors so I could cut it out. I couldn't find any. So in the end I tore it out and slipped the label inside my pocket. I was sure Giles wouldn't notice the label was missing until later. Meanwhile, when I got home I'd hide this label in a very safe place. Then tomorrow I'd go and confront him.

I'll say: 'If you want the label back you must resign from being Gracie's tutor and never go near her or her house again.'

7.25 p.m.

Giles Wallace left without seeing me. I told Gracie's mum what a rotten tutor he was, but I'm not sure she completely believed me. She said, 'This isn't a secret plot you've worked out with Gracie so she hasn't got to have a tutor, is it?'

'I've never been more shocked—' I began.

She smiled. 'I'll have to give him a chance, and then we'll see.'

Later Gracie said, 'Don't worry, I'll be watching this tutor very closely tomorrow.'

'Oh, I wouldn't do that,' I said at once. 'In fact, it'd be better if you didn't look at him at all.'

'What!' Gracie cried.

'Well, not directly; a few sideways glances will be fine, but that's all. Mainly just keep staring down at your work.'

'Why?' she demanded.

I took a deep breath. I was so worked up I could hardly speak. 'As a massive favour to me, don't make any direct eye contact with him tomorrow. Will you do that?'

'OK . . .' she began.

'And the second he leaves, ring me. I've got

no school tomorrow, either; it's an Inset day.'

'If you like, I could get Mum to drive me round to your house after he's gone.'

'Even better,' I said. 'In fact, come to mine for your lunch – and you won't forget what I've said, will you?'

She smiled. 'I really won't, Ved.'

CHAPTER TWENTY-ONE

Tuesday 13 November

11.30 p.m.
Giles Wallace's coat label has been put in an envelope and hidden under my mattress. If Giles wants it back he'll have to get past me first.

11.35 p.m.
Not that I'm expecting a late-night call from Giles.

Wednesday 14 November

7.00 a.m.
First thing I did when I woke up was to check

Giles's envelope was still under my mattress. It is. Actually, I don't think he has a clue I've got it. I wonder if he's noticed it has gone yet. It's not the sort of thing you'd check, is it? You'd just suddenly spot it had been ripped out. And that would alarm anyone. It's such a weird thing to do. But Giles would realize the significance at once. Then he'd be unnerved. And what a shock he'll get when I turn up at his house this afternoon with my ultimatum.

12.20 p.m.

Gracie should be at my house any second now. She hasn't called this morning – or replied to my text reminding her to be careful, which is unusual. Normally, she texts me all day. Still, she probably hasn't had a chance under Giles's beady eye. And anyway, I'll see her in about twenty seconds. Unless, maybe, she's gone all hairy again? But no, her mum would have called us – and anyway, we are about the only people she could visit if she was hairy again.

Then I noticed I was being watched – by my mum.

She smiled. 'Don't look so anxious.'

'I didn't know I was.'

'You like her, don't you?'

'Like who?'

'The young lady you've invited here for her lunch. I've never known you do that before. I've got a little bit of advice for you, though.'

'Now there's a surprise,' I muttered.

'You don't need to worry. Gracie likes you too.'

'Does she really, Mum? Well, thanks, you've solved all my worries now.'

'So, Marcus, when Gracie arrives – just relax.'

'Hey, Mum, that's probably the wisest thing I've heard. Good enough to print on a tea towel. Mum, you're a true philosopher.'

Very annoyingly, she just went on smiling at me.

12.45 p.m.

Still no sign of Gracie.

Meanwhile, Mum announced, 'I've got to go, but the lunch is all set up. You've just got to tuck in – I'll be back at about four o'clock. I'm sure you'll make Gracie feel at home, and—'

'I know,' I interrupted. 'Just relax.'

12.55 p.m.

Gracie really should be here by now.

A couple of minutes ago I rang her. No answer. And now I've got this massive fluttering in my stomach as if I've swallowed about ninety million butterflies. I can't believe I'm getting so worked up.

Then, with a stab of horror, I realized the strange behaviour of my stomach wasn't only because I'm worried about Gracie.

I'm about to get another blood fever attack.

1.07 p.m.

And I didn't need to see any pictures of blood this time. It just suddenly erupted. Another massive craving. So I staggered back and gulped down my 'medicine'. As before, it tasted really hot at first, but wonderful, and it just slipped down my throat so easily. I downed every last drop. Then I looked at myself in the mirror. My mouth was bright red and covered in blood. So I carefully wiped my mouth with one of those special thick handkerchiefs that I keep with me at all times now. I had to ensure not a trace of blood remained.

183

But after all that I was still thirsty. I needed to have more blood now. So what should I do? Mum had said to ring her or Dad immediately. And I knew they'd race back, thrilled that I'd had another blood fever attack so quickly. I was even a little bit excited about this myself.

But why did these attacks always come at totally the wrong time? I had to confront Giles Wallace today. Once my parents knew about the blood fever attack, they'd insist I stayed inside for the next couple of days. So I just couldn't afford to tell them yet. I had too much to do.

Then I remembered that Mum kept a little bottle of blood in the top cupboard in the kitchen for special occasions and celebrations. I only meant to have an extra sip, but it was so bloodtastic I drained the bottle. I ran the very last few drops around my mouth. You'll have to take my word on this one, blog, but there really isn't a creamier or a more delicious taste in the whole world.

Then, just as suddenly as it started, the blood fever attack was over. I wiped my mouth again and then slipped upstairs and flossed and brushed my teeth, to make sure there wasn't a trace of blood in my mouth . . . and then the doorbell rang.

1.45 p.m.

It was Gracie. 'I'm really sorry I'm so late,' she cried, 'but after the lesson Mum stayed talking to Giles for ages. I think she was trying to check if he was as rubbish a tutor as you said. And then, when we finally did get going, I forgot my phone, so I couldn't call or text you.'

'But you're all right?' I asked, staring at her anxiously.

'Of course I am. Starving hungry, though. And Mum's gone off to the shops so I can stay right through to tea time.'

I led her into the kitchen. 'My mum had to go out too, but she said to pig out as much as you like.'

Gracie saw all the food and murmured, 'Well, I shall do exactly what your mum suggested.' She sat down at the table and said casually, 'By the way, Giles isn't as bad as you said.'

'Trust me, he is.'

'No, he's a bit strict and you can't get him off the subject. I did try. And would you believe it, he's given me homework for when he's back tomorrow.'

'I wouldn't bother doing it,' I said, 'because he won't be back tomorrow.'

Gracie stared at me. 'Why won't he? Come on, tell me what's going on.'

'Nothing,' I murmured.

'And why couldn't I look directly into his eyes?'

I shifted uneasily. 'No special reason.'

But Gracie was glaring at me. 'I thought you were the one person I could trust, but now you're keeping things from me too. Really you're no better than my mum.' She stood up. 'And I've suddenly lost my appetite.'

'Oh, come on, Gracie.'

'No, I'm sick of secrets and not being told stuff!'

I could see her point completely. So I said, 'OK. If you stop flapping about I'll tell you everything.'

And I did. I hadn't planned to do this at all, but everything that had happened since

Tallulah and I had first visited Elsa just flowed out. And Gracie was listening to me open-mouthed until I told her how I'd recognized Giles at her house yesterday and stolen his coat label.

'That's really clever,' she began, but then she gave an odd little laugh and said, 'So today I was taught by a vampire who was just longing to drink my blood.'

'Well, you've seen him for the first and last time. After what I say to him this afternoon, he'll never bother you again. I won't take the label with me, though.'

'So what will you do with it?'

I thought for a moment. 'Elsa suggested leaving it with her. Giles doesn't know anything about her. And I'll say he won't get the label back until he does what I tell him and leaves the area. A vampire's pride is so strong that Elsa reckons he will do just that.' Then I added, 'I did wonder if I should have warned your mum yesterday.'

'Oh, she'd have had three nervous breakdowns at least. No, I think your way is much better. But I'm going with you to see him, of course.'

'No, you're not.'

'I certainly am. You're doing this to save my skin, so I want to be in on it too. And I shan't take no for an answer. In fact, I'll follow you anyhow.'

I looked at her. She was determined. And it wouldn't do any harm, I supposed. Also, I'd just had a blood fever attack and right now I felt fine, but later – who knows? So it might be safer to have Gracie there with me too.

And I was about to say, 'Yeah, all right,' to her when my mobile rang so loudly and suddenly it made us both jump.

I answered it, and instantly a voice whispered, 'I can't tell you how much I hate you.'

It was Tallulah.

CHAPTER TWENTY-TWO

Wednesday 14 November

1.55 p.m.

'Great talking to you too, Tallulah,' I said while she ranted on.

'You are the worst person in the entire world.'

'Have I done anything in particular to irritate you, or are you just in one of your usual bad moods? And, oh yes, why are you whispering?'

'I'm whispering because I'm at Mrs Lenchester's house.'

That gave me a jolt. 'So how is she?' I asked as casually as I could.

'Don't play innocent with me. She told me

you saw her on Monday and are off on a mission involving Giles Wallace. Mrs Lenchester wanted to know how you'd got on. She hadn't heard anything and so she emailed me. I can't believe you're doing all this without even telling me,' she screeched.

'But you're ill,' I cried.

'That's no excuse. You still should have kept me in the picture, especially as I'm in charge of everything.'

What a typical Tallulah statement *that* was: *I'm in charge of everything.*

She rushed on. 'Mrs Lenchester said you had to get something belonging to Giles; have you done that?'

'Yes.'

I heard Tallulah saying to Elsa, 'Yes, he's done that.' Then she said to me, 'Well done.'

'Thanks.'

'That "Well done" is from Mrs Lenchester, not me – I still think you're lower than something I'd scrape off my shoe.' Then she started whispering again. 'Mrs Lenchester wants you to come over right away as she's got something vital to tell you.'

'That's OK; I was coming to see her anyway.'

'Without telling me?!' Tallulah screamed.

'Look, will you stop moaning at me,' I cried. 'I'm having a highly stressful time as it is!'

'Good,' snapped Tallulah, 'and hurry up.'

I turned to Gracie. 'You probably guessed – that was Tallulah.'

'Yeah,' said Gracie softly.

'She's at Elsa's house now and I know she'll insist on going to Giles's with me.' I hesitated for a second. 'And I do think three of us might be a bit of a crowd.'

Gracie nodded quickly, but without looking at me. The atmosphere had become distinctly flat. I didn't know what else to say to her either. So in the end I dived upstairs to get the label which was still in the envelope. When I came downstairs again, Gracie was waiting by the front door.

'I knew I might not be able to come,' she said, 'because three's a crowd and all that. And anyway, Mum can't tell me when I might suddenly turn into the Bearded Girl once more! I bet that would shock him, all right. But I want you to ring me every half hour –

just so I know you're safe. Will you do that?'

'Yeah, OK.'

'Call me first at three o'clock, then every half hour. OK?'

'I'll remember.'

'Don't forget, either; I haven't got my mobile,' said Gracie, 'so you'll have to ring me on the landline.'

'That's no problem.'

'And if you don't ring me, then I'll call you, and if I don't get an answer—'

'Then I've been annihilated by a vampire.'

Gracie gasped and stepped back from me. 'That isn't funny.'

'Yes, it is. Look, I'll be fine; I've got his coat label.'

'But what if you're not?' she persisted. 'Who knows what Giles could do to you?'

'Now you're really cheering me up.'

'All right, but just in case you're in big trouble, what do I do?'

'OK, in a total, total emergency, but only then, call my mum and dad and get them to go to Elsa's house. She'll know what to do.'

'You'd better give me Elsa's address and phone number then.'

'Well, I haven't got her phone number, but look, here is her address.' I scribbled it down and said, 'This is all getting very serious – you'll have me writing my will out next.'

She grinned. 'Do that too, if you like, leaving everything to me, of course.'

I was laughing with her when I felt really unsteady for a second, as if I were about to faint. And then I had that strange churning feeling as if something was running about in the pit of my stomach. The blood fever must be kicking in again. I so hoped I wouldn't start doing those stupid animal noises again. Dr Jasper did say the effects of every blood fever attack were completely different. Anyway, I just couldn't think about that now.

Gracie was looking at me anxiously. 'Are you OK?'

'Never better,' I shouted. 'See you really soon, Gracie.'

Then I sped out of my house, and when I came to Brent Woods I just raced through there as fast as I could. I didn't want to give myself time to get scared.

At Elsa's cottage, Tallulah was waiting by

the door for me. 'You took your time,' she moaned.

'No, I didn't. And aren't you pleased to see me?'

'Never.'

Then Elsa appeared. 'Ah, here's your boyfriend. And you've been so worried about him, haven't you?'

A look of total horror crossed Tallulah's face.

'Thanks for worrying about me,' I said. 'It's great to have such a caring girlfriend, brings a warm glow to my heart.'

'Say another word and I'll throw up all over you,' hissed Tallulah.

Elsa, not hearing any of this, smiled and said, 'I've prepared you both some light refreshments before you go into the fray.'

'Oh, we haven't got time for that,' said Tallulah.

'Before you two go off, I need to make sure you've got a proper campaign plan. So please, let me do this my way.' Elsa's voice was polite but steely. And Tallulah didn't say another word.

'Now,' said Elsa, handing round cups of tea, 'the first question, Marcus, is: Have you remembered to bring what you took from the vampire with you?'

I took the coat label out of the envelope. 'There was nothing in his pockets, but this will have his smell on it, won't it?'

'Very powerfully,' said Elsa. 'And the fact that you have taken it is deeply humiliating for a vampire.'

'It was a bit of a weird coincidence, actually,' I said. 'I was visiting a friend who'd been ill and she said a tutor was popping in – and it was Giles.'

'I don't believe in coincidences,' says Elsa. 'So just as I believe I was meant to pick up Tallulah's message on the internet that day, I believe that you, Marcus, were meant to be involved in this. It's your destiny,' she added gravely.

'And mine,' Tallulah practically shouted. 'So now do we go and wave this label in his face?' she added eagerly.

'Oh no,' said Elsa Lenchester firmly. 'Then he will merely use his powers to get it back from you. And don't ever underestimate a vampire's power or cunning. I will keep this here for now.'

'But then we'd be putting you in danger,' I said.

Elsa chuckled. 'Oh, I haven't lasted this long without being able to look after myself. I'll be fine.'

'Just hit him with your stick if he comes near you,' said Tallulah.

'That's no protection against a vampire mad with fury,' I said. 'I don't think we can ask you—'

'You're very kind,' interrupted Elsa, 'but I'd like to play my part in this adventure. So, please let me. And anyway, this Giles Wallace doesn't associate you two with me at all, does he?'

'That's true,' said Tallulah, looking at me. 'And as I'm the leader of this mission, I'm telling you to hand it over, Marcus.'

I still felt very uneasy, though. Elsa was an old lady living in this pretty isolated spot all alone. No one seemed to look out for her, either. Right then I decided that when this vampire was caught I'd still come and see Elsa.

My grannies are great, but they are so busy and confident. Elsa was much closer to the kind of granny I'd always wanted. And she makes great biscuits too. What more could you want?

'Now listen carefully,' said Elsa. 'Knock on the vampire's door and tell him you have his coat label – describe it carefully so he knows you're telling him the truth. He probably won't have noticed its absence yet. Then say: "The game is up and your time is over." He'll know exactly what that means. Then offer to either return the label or to destroy it. He probably won't want it back.'

At the door she said to us, 'I so wish I could come with you. And inside my head and heart I will be there beside you.'

'Just remember,' I said, 'only answer the door to us, no one else.'

Then, as we raced towards Giles's house, Tallulah announced, 'By the way, I'm doing all the talking.'

I stared at her with a mixture of puzzlement and awe. 'You're really not scared at all, are you?'

'Why should I be?' Tallulah answered. 'I just know this is going to be the best moment of my whole life.'

CHAPTER TWENTY-THREE

Wednesday 14 November

2.40 p.m.

We rang Giles's doorbell. And he opened the door immediately. He had an exercise book in his hand – to keep up his pose as a tutor, I suppose – and he blinked at us in astonishment.

'But you're not who I'm expecting at all.' Then he gave me one of his stupidly thin smiles. 'Well, my young friend – you do keep popping up, don't you? And you've brought your young lady with you this time as well.'

Tallulah gulped furiously at this description of herself, while he purred on, 'So what on earth can I do for you? I am rather busy just now, actually.'

'We have something of yours,' said Tallulah grimly.

'But how intriguing,' he said, lightly scratching his moustache. 'Whatever can it be?'

'The label off your coat,' said Tallulah. 'Marcus tore it off yesterday.'

Then I added, 'It says *Modina* and it's quite a large label.'

'I have my coat right here.' He returned with it, then peered inside. Elsa was right; he hadn't had a clue until now that the label had been removed. I stepped ever so slightly back, afraid he might turn vicious suddenly. But instead he just looked totally bewildered and confused. And his voice went very whiny. 'Why on earth would you do that?'

'We're keeping the label for you in a safe place,' said Tallulah, 'and you can have it back later. We have a message for you too,' she continued. 'The game is up and your time is over. I'm told you'll know exactly what that means.'

Giles's face – in fact his whole body – now

199

grew very still. 'I did wonder . . . but I never . . .' he began. Then he stopped and said in a low, flat voice, 'I suppose you'd better come in.'

Tallulah and I looked at each other. Elsa hadn't said anything about going inside his house. What should we do?

'Well, we will step inside,' said Tallulah, 'but don't even think of trying anything. We have people who know we're here – very powerful people.' I smiled faintly at the idea of Elsa as a very powerful person, but Tallulah was quite right to say it.

Giles led us into a room in which there was a large table heaped with books and papers, but otherwise it had an odd sense that some-one hadn't properly moved in yet. The blinds weren't drawn, either. But then, being a vampire, Giles wouldn't be keen on the after-noon light.

So we both stood facing Giles in this dim, dark room. Tallulah said sternly, 'We have a further message for you. It is vital you leave this house today and never return. When we're satisfied you have done this, the label will be returned or destroyed, but not before.'

Giles stared at us accusingly. 'I never suspected you,' he whispered.

'Well, you should have done,' said Tallulah.

'You shouldn't ever underestimate teenagers,' I added, while all the time watching Giles extremely carefully. For this was too easy. Surely Giles wasn't just going to give up like that.

'I just don't understand why you are helping them,' he said softly. 'It's me you should be helping.'

'I know,' said Tallulah, sounding more than a bit regretful. 'And I do admire vampires in so many ways, but still, you have been doing some very bad stuff—'

'But I'm not a vampire,' he interrupted.

'Oh come on, mate, cut the act,' I said. 'You've been rumbled. Tallulah and me know all about vampires, you know.'

'No, no,' he said. 'You're wrong. Not about there being vampires – and it's refreshing to see two young people prepared to put themselves in danger to defeat a monstrous evil most people won't even *believe* exists. But I'm not a vampire. I'm a vampire *hunter* – and you've just put me in the gravest danger.'

CHAPTER TWENTY-FOUR

Wednesday 14 November

2.45 p.m.

What Giles had said wasn't right at all. It couldn't be.

'We're not falling for that,' I said.

'I can prove it,' he began. But then he clasped both his hands to his stomach, as if he'd just eaten something disgusting. He pitched forward, doubled up in pain.

I stood watching him very sceptically. 'Now what's going on?'

'Just before you came in, I felt suddenly off-colour, but now – now it's really started.'

'What has?' demanded Tallulah.

He gave a choked cry of agony and then fell

back onto a chair. Tallulah rushed over and crouched down beside Giles as if she were really concerned about him.

'Don't look into his eyes, Tallulah,' I hissed. 'This is a trap.'

She glared up at me. 'Shut up!' And then she actually stared right at him. 'What's happened to you? Please, you must tell us.'

Giles drew a long breath and then said in a croaky whisper, 'Certain vampires, once they are given something belonging to their victim, can saturate that person with their power. And they can even set a spell to suck my blood, just as surely as if they'd swooped on me. Only a few vampires can do this. And I believe you've given my coat label to one of the most deadly and powerful of them all . . . the one I trailed here. It is vital you tell me this vampire's identity.'

'Oh yeah, right,' I said, and then I started to laugh. Nice, kind, frail Elsa in her flowery dresses and squeaky slippers a deadly vampire? That was the maddest, stupidest, most ridiculous thing I'd ever heard.

'But she – or he,' added Tallulah quickly, 'is

the one who told us about vampires being nearby.'

Giles didn't answer at first. He was too busy coughing. Then he gasped, 'The vampire senses a vampire hunter has moved here recently. He needs to find me, but can't show his hand directly. So he gets you to do it for him. Then he wants to cast a spell on me to put me out of action, but he can't do that without one of my belongings, which he now has.'

'Thanks to us,' gasped Tallulah.

'You must stop this vampire.' Giles's voice was croaky, pleading.

'But how do we do that?' asked Tallulah.

'It's very simple,' he managed. 'Get the label back. Only do it right away. And be very, very careful. This vampire is just brimming with poison.'

'Yeah, right,' I said.

Giles was struggling to say something else, but instead let out a yell of pain. I sneaked another look at him, getting ready to duck away if he tried to hold my gaze. His mouth was opening and shutting like a fish which had just been hauled out of the sea. But it was his eyes I noticed most of all. They looked as if they were about to pop right out of his head. You could almost believe invisible fangs really were squeezing more and more blood from him!

'Top acting,' I said, very sarcastically.

Tallulah stared gravely at him and then pronounced, like a doctor giving a medical verdict, 'He really *is* ill. He's not acting.'

'Of course he is. And we won't leave here until he tells us what he's really up to.'

But Tallulah sprang up, grabbed my arm with both her hands and shook me. 'Wake up, Marcus, he's telling the truth.'

'No, this is a trap, I know it is.'

'And I know it isn't.' Then, more to herself than me: 'I should have seen through her before. But of course . . .' She crouched down beside Giles. 'The vampire is Elsa Lenchester, who lives in one of those cottages up the end of the road. I let her fool me, but don't worry,' she said, more gently than I'd ever heard her talk to anyone, 'we won't let you down. We'll get your label back and we'll run like lightning too.' Then, to my huge surprise, she gave him a little pat on the shoulder. 'Just hang on in there.' Then she whispered something to him which I couldn't catch. After which she turned to me. 'So, am I going on my own?'

'You're making a massive mistake,' I said. 'But OK, I'll go with you.'

We tore back to Elsa's house then. Or rather, Tallulah did, though she had to stop once to have a bit of a coughing fit.

I kept stopping and looking over my shoulder. 'I still think we should check he's not following us.'

'Following us? Marcus, what are you talking about? That poor guy can barely speak now, let alone move. And he's not acting.'

'And I tell you he is and he's a total phoney. Doesn't my opinion count for anything?'

'No.' I glanced back again.

'Spotted him yet?' asked Tallulah, with a definite edge of sarcasm in her voice. 'You've got to believe me, Elsa is the vampire. I bet her husband Fungus was one too.'

'Fergus,' I corrected. 'And you're so wrong.' Then I added, 'And what did you whisper to him when you were leaving?'

'Oh, I just told him help was on the way or

something like that,' said Tallulah vaguely.

Just ahead of us now was Elsa's little cottage.

'Here's the plan,' whispered Tallulah. 'We tell Elsa we've confronted Giles and told him to leave in the next twenty-four hours – so she'll think we believe he is a vampire.'

'I still do,' I muttered.

'Then we'll very innocently ask for the label back. If she lets us have it—'

'Then Giles has been conning us,' I interrupted.

'Yes, OK, calm down,' said Tallulah. 'But whatever happens we won't leave until we get that label back. We can't do anything else, can we?'

I hesitated. My stomach gave a lurch, just as if something was clawing away inside me. I felt giddy for a moment.

'Can we?' repeated Tallulah, looking at me expectantly.

'No,' I agreed quietly, 'we can't.'

And then Tallulah banged on Elsa's cottage door.

CHAPTER TWENTY-FIVE

Friday 16 November

11.30 a.m.

Two whole days have gone by since my last blog.

It was straight after this that the terror really began. And my whole world came crashing down around my ears. But at last I'm ready to tell you everything.

So let's go back to Wednesday afternoon, when Tallulah and I were waiting outside Elsa's cottage. I remember she was ages answering the door.

'She's done a runner,' said Tallulah.

'Behave, she can barely hobble, let alone run,' I said.

'Well, where is she?'

'There.' I pointed. And just behind the glass we could see Elsa tottering towards us. And when she opened the door her face was, as usual, alight with friendliness.

'Oh, splendid, you're safe,' she cried, 'and you have news, I can tell. Well, come in, my dears. I want to hear everything.'

We piled into Elsa's sitting room. And soon Tallulah was rattling away about how we'd just confronted Giles. And you'd never have guessed she suspected Elsa at all. She was playing it exactly right.

Tallulah went on, 'Giles tried to trick us by pretending he was ill. But we weren't fooled by that. And I'm certain he knows the game is up.'

'How well you've done,' said Elsa. 'Acting with a maturity well beyond your years. Well, I think this calls for a celebratory cup of tea.'

'Actually, Mrs Lenchester . . .' Tallulah began.

'Please, my dear,' she said gently, 'it's Elsa.'

'All right, Elsa, we've got to leave now,' said Tallulah. 'I'm not supposed to be out this long.' She coughed.

'Of course, you're still quite ill, aren't you?' Elsa said in a worried voice.

'But before we go we'd just like the label back, please,' said Tallulah. 'We can look after it now.'

'It's not fair,' I chipped in, 'to put the responsibility on to you.'

There was a beat of silence. I swallowed hard, and then Elsa said, 'Of course, my dears. I'll just get it for you.'

She left and I couldn't help muttering to Tallulah, 'See, no problem. I bet Giles is laughing his head off at us.' Then, rubbing it in, 'Who knows what he's planning now?'

Tallulah didn't answer, just kept her head down, frowning.

Elsa came shuffling back. 'Do you know, I've put that label in such a safe place in the kitchen that I can't find it. I know you're in a hurry to be off, so I'll have a proper search for it, and if you'd be so kind as to wait until tomorrow, I'll certainly have found it for you by then. I'm very sorry to have temporarily lost it.' Her voice was so gentle and reasonable, but a little chill still ran through me.

Tallulah jumped to her feet and said

firmly, 'I'm sorry, but we really must have that label now.'

'Of course, of course,' said Elsa. 'Look, don't worry; I'll have another thorough look in the kitchen. You just sit here and relax for a moment. I shan't be long, my dears.'

As soon as she'd left Tallulah announced, 'And I shall have a thorough search in here. Let's start with this desk.' She started flinging open the drawers.

'Tallulah, I really don't think—' I began.

'I'm doing it, not you,' she snapped. 'These drawers feel really heavy.'

'It won't be in there,' I said.

Tallulah didn't answer. She was now peering into the third drawer. Then she pounced and started waving a small label madly in the air. 'Marcus, this is it, isn't it?' she began.

I nodded.

Stunned by this discovery, I didn't see a small shadow creep in through the doorway. In fact, the first I knew that we were not alone was when a screaming ball of tortoiseshell fur and teeth hurled itself at Tallulah, sending the label in her hand flying to the ground. A stunned Tallulah flailed backwards.

'Hey, are you all right?' I said, rushing over to her.

'Yes, yes,' she said, quickly brushing herself down. 'That crazy thing just took me by surprise. We've got to get that label back and then run like mad out of here.'

But the label was now right beside Rufus. In fact, the cat seemed to be standing guard over it, his tail swishing from side to side.

'I'll try and get it,' I said.

I stared at the cat and his huge green eyes instantly locked onto mine. And then he started spitting furiously. I felt if I moved another millimetre he would leap forward and rip me apart. I turned to Tallulah. 'This is not going to be easy.'

'But we have to get it back,' whispered Tallulah, 'otherwise Giles . . .' And her voice trailed away, not really wanting to finish that sentence.

'Maybe if we both charge at the cat together,' I suggested.

'No, hopeless, quite hopeless,' said a cold, hard voice behind us, making me jump. There was Elsa standing in the doorway, coolly watching us. 'Rufus would never let

212

you leave this room alive. Better than any guard dog, aren't you? So we'll let him keep that ridiculous label for now.' Then she looked at us and shook her head.

'Elsa, what's going on?' I asked in a slow, trembling voice, still hoping there'd be some explanation from her.

She didn't answer at first. Instead, she strode over to her desk and slammed shut the drawers that Tallulah had opened. Then Elsa smacked the desk top with such ferocious anger we both jumped back from her. And right then it hit me like a gunshot, how totally Elsa had deceived me.

'Oh, why did you have to be so nosy?' she said, shaking her head at us. And suddenly she seemed years – no, *decades* younger. Not a frail, old lady at all but a . . .

'You really are a vampire, aren't you?' cried Tallulah.

'Of course I am,' said Elsa proudly. 'And you know those dangerous vampires I warned you about? Well, I'm the worst one of all.'

CHAPTER TWENTY-SIX

I gaped at Elsa. It was just as if she'd been wearing a mask which she'd suddenly flung away. That kindly, fluttery old-lady look had vanished from her face, leaving someone with no expression at all. Staring at her eyes was like looking at two black buttons. They were cold, dead and drained of any feeling at all.

'Well, I've had my fun,' said Elsa. 'Now I've got to decide what to do with you two miserable specimens.'

'You're not doing anything with us,' I said, as bravely as I could.

'No, you can't keep us here,' cried Tallulah.

'I have no wish to keep you here,' said Elsa. 'In fact, I can't think of anything I'd like less. You will both leave here very shortly.'

'Will we?' Tallulah was stunned. So was I.

'You have my word on that,' said Elsa.

'But what's that worth?' demanded Tallulah, moving closer to her.

'Of course, when you leave I'll have burned out all your memories of what's happened here. In fact, you'll be lucky if you remember your own names.'

I was still frozen with shock. I'd been so sure of Elsa's innocence that my brain wasn't working properly yet. But Tallulah marched right up to her.

'You're just evil, aren't you?' She almost spat the words. I had to admire Tallulah's bravery.

'Now don't go showering me with compliments,' said Elsa.

'You can't keep us here,' declared Tallulah again.

'Can't I?' Elsa's voice was teasing, almost playful.

'No, we're going to leave – and with Giles's label.'

'Are you?' purred Elsa. She didn't seem at all bothered by what Tallulah was saying and seemed, in fact, to be encouraging her to say more.

Then, with a stab of horror, I came to life and realized why. I yelled out, 'Tallulah! You're looking right into her eyes. Move away fast.'

But it was too late. The very next second Tallulah's head began to sway. And then she dropped to the ground like a puppet whose strings had all been cut. I sped to her side. She was crouched on the ground on her knees, her head swinging slightly from side to side and her eyes glazed.

'Hey, what have you done to her?' I demanded of Elsa.

'She's going under one of my spells,' said Elsa. 'I'm putting her in a deep trance.'

'No, you're not,' I shouted. I knew a bit about these vampire trances. If other voices were heard, it stopped the trance from being so deep. So I yelled and shouted, 'Tallulah! Stay awake! . . . Go on, you can do it!'

Tallulah raised her head for a moment.

I crouched down beside her. 'Come on, fight it.'

Her eyes were far away like a sleepwalker's.

She didn't look like Tallulah at all. It was horrible. But very slowly she moved her head again for a moment.

'All right, you've stopped the trance going so deep,' said Elsa. 'But she'll still be under for about fifteen minutes – which will be long enough. Now, leave her alone.'

But I went on, 'Tallulah, maybe you can still hear me a bit. Well, I'll get us out of this, so just . . . well, don't worry, and oh yeah, you were totally right about Elsa Lenchester.'

Then I got to my feet as Elsa gave a sort of laugh. 'You so wanted me to be a gentle, fluttery old nan, didn't you?' Then, seeing my surprised look, she went on, 'Vampires can see not only your nightmares but your pathetic little dreams too. So I pretended to be what you wanted. And didn't I play the part well.'

I felt too humiliated and let down to even reply.

She went on, 'Of course, the moment you arrived I knew instantly what you were.' She shook her head contemptuously. 'If we're creatures of the night, what are you? Creatures of the . . . when it's just starting to get dark?'

So she'd guessed my secret identity right away. I quickly turned to Tallulah, but she was far away in her trance now. Following my eyes, Elsa Lenchester said, 'Oh, I'll tell that brat what you are before I've finished with her, which should bring me some extra fun.'

Suddenly a new sound erupted through the room . . . my mobile phone. I knew immediately who it was: Gracie. I'd totally forgotten to ring her at three o'clock, like I'd said I would. And now she was calling me, just like *she'd* said. So here it was: my chance – my only chance – to get help.

That's why I had to answer that phone. Only Elsa wasn't going to let me do that.

Then my stomach gave another lurch as if to remind me I wasn't entirely myself. And after my first blood fever attack I'd been hyper-strong for a brief while, even fighting off a vampire in the wood. With a stab of shock I suddenly realized who that vampire must have been – Elsa Lenchester.

But if I could fight Elsa before, I could do it again. And anyway, I only had to talk to Gracie very briefly. Just tell her to ring my

218

parents and get them to race round here. I could say all that really fast. And once I'd told Gracie . . . well, Elsa wouldn't dare do anything, would she?

The phone carried on ringing.

'Such an ugly sound,' said Elsa. 'And of course, that's one call I can never let you answer.' She sounded so confident and amused, it was really bugging me. Well, I was about to wipe that self-satisfied smirk off her face. But it was only her lips which were smiling. Her eyes remained as cold and as dead as those of a shark.

But I couldn't let this chance slip away. I reached into my pocket.

'Stop now – or you'll be very sorry.' Her voice was like a whiplash.

But I didn't hesitate. I knew I had to go on. I pulled the phone out and I'd just touched the switch when Elsa made her move. In one giant leap she was across the room. A firm hand grabbed me by the shoulder, shaking me madly until I relaxed my grip on the phone which went skidding across the room.

Then Elsa gave this weird, bird-like cry and before I knew it she was tearing at my face and body with such speed my eyes could not keep up with her. Definitely time for me to fight back, just as I'd done in the wood. Only that mega-strength I could call on last time wasn't there. And I wasn't able to stop her at all. In the end, with a hand that was more like a claw, she knocked me backwards. And I went crashing into the wall by the door.

I lay there, struggling to breathe. I'd had all the air knocked out of me.

I tried to move, while she gave this odd screech of triumph, only my right knee was agonizingly painful. In fact, it just exploded with pain. I must have twisted it. And my whole body ached. Then a spine-chilling howl of joy burst across the room, while my phone continued to wail piteously. It suddenly sounded very scared.

Then Rufus stalked over to me.

'Dear Rufus,' said Elsa, 'always taking such an interest, but don't touch him just yet.' She stood gloating over me. 'That was so foolish of you,' she said.

Anger and frustration reared up inside me. Why couldn't I have fought as I had the last time I was attacked, especially when so much depended on it now? But then I remembered something Dr Jasper had said: the effects of each blood fever attack are different. One time I might be a kind of warrior, the next I could temporarily read minds or . . . or I could send messages to someone close to me.

In a flash, another idea hit me. Could I send a message to Gracie now? If I could contact anyone telepathically, it would be her.

It was worth a try anyway. I shut my eyes. *Gracie, this is Marcus and I need to contact you urgently.* And as I said this inside my head something whirled about in my vision. It was like my own little private firework display. Was that a sign I could do this, or just a delayed reaction to falling against the wall? I had to be hopeful.

So then I transmitted a message to Gracie without saying a word. I was speaking to her from inside my head: *Gracie, I hope you can hear me. Tallulah and I are in grave danger. Elsa Lenchester is the vampire! Call my mum or dad now and get them to come urgently to her cottage. You remember, I wrote the address down.*

Act now, Gracie. You're our only hope.

CHAPTER TWENTY-SEVEN

I opened my eyes to see Elsa Lenchester peering down at me. I remembered to duck away from her gaze.

'Now if you co-operate, it won't be too bad,' she said.

'Yes, it will. You're going to drain my mind of all my memories of everything that makes me . . . *me*.'

Elsa Lenchester didn't deny this. In fact, she said proudly, 'I do get a bit over-enthusiastic. Still, you haven't got any choice really. *She* certainly can't help you.' She nodded over at Tallulah, who was still crouched on her knees, lost in a trance. Fury boiled up inside me, not only with Elsa but also with myself.

Why hadn't I thought to ring Gracie before I'd come back to this cottage? When I'd agreed to call her? Then I could have said: *If I don't ring you back in fifteen minutes, get help right away.* Instead I'd just blundered in here because I wouldn't even consider the possibility that Giles was telling the truth and Elsa was the vampire. I had so wanted to believe that Elsa was this sweet old lady that I'd totally fallen for her lies. And now we were trapped here, totally at a vampire's mercy.

A vampire's mercy! There was no such thing.

This was a nightmare, all right.

And only one person could get us out of this: Gracie. I just hoped she'd somehow picked up my message – and alerted my parents to Elsa's true identity.

Gracie would have to be fast too. For if Tallulah and I were hypnotized and drained of all memories – well, then Gracie would just be rescuing two zombies. My heart started to thump violently.

Somehow I had to at least delay Elsa. But how? And then something Dad said came

223

floating up. He had said that vampires' only weaknesses are their pride and their vanity.

'You really fooled me, you know,' I said to Elsa. 'I believed totally that you were just a nice old lady.'

'Well, I *was* an actress, of course,' said Elsa proudly. For a moment she even seemed to forget about me and be staring right back into her past as she added, 'A very good actress too, and if I'd had the breaks, Fergus said I'd have gone right to the top, as I could tackle any role really: drama one week, high comedy the next.'

'I can believe that,' I said.

'Fergus said I had real star quality. I could have been one of the top vampires too, if they'd had eyes . . . and seen what I was offering. But they never really accepted me or Fergus. He was a vampire too. And his knowledge was truly incredible. He tracked down things . . .'

'Including that chain you gave us to detect vampires?' I asked.

'Oh no, that was one hundred per cent fake,' replied Elsa, sweeping around the room and revelling in her own cleverness. 'The

224

chain just happens to get warm every so often. But I needed something to keep you busy. That stupid girl had discovered what I was up to in Brent Woods on her vampire website. It was vital I moved her attention onto something else. Then I sensed this new-comer – this vampire hunter. So I decided I'd get you to find out who he was for me. It amused me to pretend he was a vampire. But I thought after a while you'd discover the chain was worthless. So, as well as sending you those nightmares I also got you to sleep-walk over to your bedroom window and throw that chain down to me, where I was waiting. I knew the loss of it would distract you both further' – she gave her dry laugh – 'while all the time, of course, I was continuing with highly important work of my own.'

'Which was?' I asked, determined to keep her talking.

But she didn't need much prompting. 'When I came here I had lost my beloved Fergus and was very ill myself. Vampires can slow down the ageing process but they can't stop it. Not even very powerful vampires like me. And a few weeks ago I was just as frail as I pretended to be with you. Then, in desperation really, I helped myself to some human blood one night, which we all shun because it tastes so absolutely rotten, but I drank it down like medicine every day for a week. No vampire I know of had ever tried to study the effect of human blood on us over a planned series of days. Oh, many tried it once or twice, and half-vampires' blood has a particular appeal at one stage in your change, as I believe you know. But this was different; this was a real experiment. It was dear Fergus's great idea, you know. And on the fifth day – well, the years started to fall away. I knew then that I'd made a truly sensational discovery.'

'So those attacks in Brent Woods . . .'

'Oh, all me,' she said cheerfully. 'And now, after each one, not only do I feel even younger but much, much stronger too. Who'd have thought such a despised taste could hold such restorative powers? But I can fight again just as I did when I was in my twenties. In fact, I'm probably even better than I was then.'

'But the humans you fed off were in quite a bad way for ages?'

She waved a dismissive hand. 'They're totally unimportant. My only regret is that I didn't make such a discovery before.' She smiled faintly. 'Why, with this new power we could have the whole world terrified of us. And we wouldn't need to hide ourselves away from miserable puny humans either. So I'm going to set up my own little group of deadly vampires who will test out and prove my theory. This sleepy little place is going to become the epicentre of the most important experiment ever.'

One of the cats started to howl.

'Yes, all right, I know you're hungry, my dears, and so am I.' I opened my mouth to ask another question, but Elsa clapped her hands. 'Enough chat – time for action.' She moved slowly but confidently towards me. 'Now, just look into my eyes.'

I turned my head away. 'I just wanted to ask you . . .' I persisted.

'Come on, look at me – it's hopeless to resist.'

I closed my eyes tightly and whispered, 'Oh, Gracie, where are you?'

And at that very moment there came three

raps on the front door, really sharp and loud. For one awful moment I thought: I've wanted to hear this sound so badly I must have just imagined it. But then I saw Elsa stiffen too. 'It's only one of my neighbours,' she said.

'Come to borrow a cup of blood?' I said. 'No, I don't think so. It's my parents come to find me. I did leave them your address, you know.'

'Nice try, but no sale,' said Elsa, but a little of the confidence had ebbed out of her voice.

'Hey, I'm in here, Dad!' I shouted.

'They'll never hear you; we're cut off from the outside world here,' snapped Elsa. 'And make another sound and you'll be very sorry. That's a promise.' And her eyes were so empty, so totally and completely without any feeling, that you felt she could do absolutely anything to you without a glimmer of concern.

There was silence then. And I thought: Surely my parents hadn't given up and gone away?

But suddenly a crisp and authoritative voice shouted through the letter box. 'Open up at once, this is the police!'

I don't know who was more stunned: Elsa

Lenchester, or me. Probably Gracie couldn't contact my parents so she'd rung the police instead. Half-vampires generally avoid involving the police in any of their business, but this was an emergency. So she'd had no choice.

Elsa's eyes were suddenly darting everywhere like a trapped animal.

It wasn't so much that she was scared of the police. It was just the total humiliation of a vampire being stopped in its tracks by a lowly human being. And the moment the police saw Tallulah lying semi-conscious on the floor Elsa would be arrested and led away. This would certainly make her an object of great ridicule in the vampire world.

'Open up now,' shouted the policewoman. 'We have received a very serious complaint about you. And if you don't open the door immediately, we shall enter by force.'

It was then I gave a splutter of shock and swallowed down my laughter. I knew that policewoman's voice.

It was Gracie.

CHAPTER TWENTY-EIGHT

It was such a brilliant impersonation that it was only now I realized the truth. Clever Gracie. What an actress! No wonder she wanted to go on the stage. But if she was pretending to be a policewoman, did that mean she was actually outside on her own? It almost certainly did. It also meant that no police officers – or anyone else, for that matter – were going to break down Elsa Lenchester's door and rescue us.

So really, it was just a massive bluff. Still, it looked as if Elsa was falling for it. But for how much longer? It was up to me to do something fast. But what? The answer hit me in a flash.

I said to Elsa, 'The police are about to rescue me. So, to quote you: the game is up and your time is over.'

Then I started to scramble to my feet, ignoring the shots of pain rushing through my right knee. I couldn't let anything stop me now.

'I will tell you when to get up,' said Elsa.

But anger fizzed furiously in my blood, and I shouted back, 'No, you won't – not with the police ready to break your door down at any moment.'

And right then there was a massive bang as the 'police' kicked at the door. 'Two minutes, Mrs Lenchester, before we break this door down.'

I have to say, Gracie was really good. And I yelled, 'So you're about to be arrested, Mrs Lenchester. Has a vampire ever been arrested before? And how humiliating is that? What's that line you quoted to me once? "Pride lost – all lost."' I was getting to her now all right. So I said it again. 'Pride lost – all lost.'

All at once Elsa let out this low, growling noise deep in her throat. It reminded me a bit of some of the noises I'd made that night in the bus shelter after I'd had blood fever. Well, we were vaguely related, and what a disgusting thought that was! But her sounds were much wilder and nastier. This was the sound of an animal that would gnaw your head off without a moment's hesitation.

But I was too fired up to stop now. And I rushed over to Tallulah and whispered, 'The bad news is, you've been put in a trance, but it'll wear off soon.'

Tallulah very slowly lifted her head. She was fighting her hardest to wake up. Suddenly her eyes sprang open and she looked straight at me.

'The even worse news is,' I whispered, 'that you've got to put your arms around me.'

And do you know, Tallulah actually gave a ragged kind of laugh. Finally she was laughing at one of my jokes. It was just a shame she was only half-conscious at the time.

So I bent down and picked up Tallulah. She held onto me surprisingly tightly. And her eyes were blinking furiously. I knew she was really trying her hardest to stay awake now.

'Soon have you out of here,' I murmured.

And then I heard Elsa make another of those creepy animal noises. What was she planning? Was she about to launch another attack on us? I had my back to her, so I couldn't see what she was doing. To keep my nerves up I started whistling softly and totally out of tune. Then I saw Tallulah was trying to say something.

'L . . .' she spluttered. She seemed really agitated.

'You want to go to the loo?' I said, thinking she really did pick her moments. Tallulah shook her head angrily – even half-conscious, it didn't take much to get her mad.

Then even my slow brain realized what she was trying to say: 'Label.' The very thing we'd come into this mad house to try and retrieve and, of course, I'd totally forgotten about it.

But there it lay on the ground. And, still with my back to Mrs Lenchester, I edged forward, whistling away. Just one problem – Rufus was crouched right in front of it.

'This label doesn't belong here and we're going to take it back to its owner,' I explained rather pointlessly to the cat. So I crouched down, still holding Tallulah, of course, and scooped up the label. Rufus began to hiss and spit as I touched it. I was ready for him to spring at me. And if that happened I decided I'd just tear out of here with Tallulah and come back for the label later.

But then a scream erupted through the room – a scream so wild and desperate it made Rufus run for his life. Suddenly I realized why Elsa had let out this cry. She'd picked up Gracie's scent: the whiff of a half-vampire who hasn't yet changed over. No smell is more potent for a vampire.

But Elsa was also more confused than ever. She couldn't work out how a half-vampire in that delicious state could be so close by. It was impossible. So was she going mad, losing all her faculties?

I had to play on this, as on no account must Elsa actually see Gracie. For then not only would Elsa know that the whole thing was a whopping great bluff, but also that a delicious-smelling half-vampire had actually walked into her home.

So I yelled out, 'The shame and humili-ation when the police break in here. And I'm going to tell them you're a vampire. Totally expose you as a nasty, scheming, vicious vampire whose powers are suddenly waning. The game's up for you, Elsa!'

Never have I shouted anything with more strength. Elsa was bent right over now, her hands shaking furiously. She was ageing before my eyes, going back to what she'd been like before she drank that blood.

Now she just looked like an incredibly ancient doddery old lady, but with one important difference. White slime was also drooling and frothing all down her chin. My stomach twisted with horror. And then a strange kind of mould crawled over her face. Moments later she began shrivelling away into the dim darkness.

I whispered to Tallulah, 'We've done it.' And without waiting around another second we just pelted out of that cottage and stepped outside to Gracie jumping all around me. But I was steering Gracie as quickly as I could, right away from that cottage. At the same moment, a car driven at ferocious speed tore into the little road. And charging out of it came my dad.

After a few garbled explanations, Dad –
who looked deathly white – carefully helped
Tallulah into the back of the car. She was still
struggling to stay awake. I sat beside her
while Gracie and Dad got in the front.

And it seemed totally unreal that I should
be in the back of Dad's car, where I'd been
hundreds of times before, after all that had
happened.

Gracie turned round and grinned at me.
She was a bit pleased with herself and
deserved to be as well.

'Well done, PC Gracie – you even fooled me
at first,' I said. Then I whispered, 'So you
picked up my message then?'

Looking at Tallulah, Gracie replied in a
very low voice, 'Well, you never rang me
as you promised: typical boy, that is. So I
called you. And when I didn't get an answer
I was a bit uneasy. But I don't know if I'd
have gone to the cottage if' – and here she
lowered her voice even further – 'if I hadn't
picked up the strongest feeling that you were
in great danger, and I had to get you out of
that cottage right away. So I called your dad,
said how I thought you might be trapped in a

house by a vampire – and then dived into a taxi here myself.'

'Will you keep your voices down,' hissed Dad. 'There's a human in the car.' And Tallulah stirred as he said that.

Whispering now, I said, 'By the way, Dad, Giles Wallace – the guy we thought was a vampire – was in a really bad way when we last saw him.'

'Unsurprising really,' snapped Dad, 'as I understand you gave one of his possessions to a vampire.'

'But will Giles be all right now?' I asked.

'Have you got the coat label back?'

I reached into my pocket. 'Safe as anything.'

'Well then, he is out of danger, but no thanks to your meddling,' began Dad.

And then Tallulah's eyes opened wide and she said, 'That label, please give it to me. I promised Giles I'd return it to him personally.'

'He doesn't need it,' I began. 'It's enough—'

'Please,' cried Tallulah. 'I promised him.' So that was what she'd whispered to him just before we'd left his house. I gave her the label. She clasped it tightly, and then closed her eyes again.

A few minutes later we dropped Tallulah off at her house, leaving her parents fluttering round her anxiously and her mum saying, 'I told her not to go out today. I knew she wasn't strong enough yet.'

Back in the car the atmosphere had turned distinctly chilly. 'We told you to stay away from vampires. So what do you do?'

'I'm sorry,' I began. Then I added, 'I realize, Dad, this hasn't made it one of my better days and I just want to say—'

'Don't say anything, will you,' said Dad. 'I can't trust myself to speak to you right now. So, not another word. Not one.'

Gracie and I exchanged looks, but neither of us dared speak. I'd never seen Dad so worked up before – and upset. Really upset.

Finally Dad demanded, 'I don't suppose there's anything else you've forgotten to tell me?'

'Just one thing,' I said lightly. 'I had another blood fever attack today.'

Dad jolted forward and nearly crashed the car with shock. 'What – but that's fantastic news.' And there was a massive smile on his face for about four seconds. Then it vanished. 'You went out after a blood fever attack when we expressly told you—'

'But I had no choice, did I?' I interrupted. Then I added: 'That's probably how I was able to send that message to Gracie, wasn't it?'

'It was,' he replied.

'So does that mean I'm going to be a genius half-vampire?'

'Let's not get carried away,' said Dad, 'but you've had quite a day.'

'Yeah,' I said. 'It has been pretty busy, hasn't it?'

CHAPTER TWENTY-NINE

Friday 16 November

4.15 p.m.

Just one last thing to tell you about the past forty-eight hours.

Today I went back with Dad to Mrs Lenchester's madhouse. Well, I'd left my phone there, hadn't I? Dad had planned to pick it up on his own, but I asked if I could come along too. I wanted to check that Elsa had really gone for ever. So Dad agreed.

It was bucketing down with rain when we set off. And just rushing out of the car to her cottage we got drenched. Still, I couldn't walk that fast on my right foot anyway.

But the door to the cottage pushed open

easily enough. 'No one's been here since . . .' began Dad and then hesitated.

'Since Tallulah and I nearly got brain-washed,' I chipped in helpfully.

Dad and I crept about that cottage like burglars. Only no cats jumped out at us today. Had they all fled somewhere? Or were they hiding, getting ready to pounce on us when we least expected it. Nothing seemed to have been taken from the sitting room at all. It was exactly as I remembered it.

And there on the floor was my mobile phone. I stared at it for a moment as if it was suddenly going to jump in the air or something.

'Well, go on, take it,' urged Dad. 'It is yours.' I knew he wanted to get out of there as quickly as possible.

Actually, so did I. That stale, musty smell seemed even thicker today. What was it Giles Wallace had said about vampires? They're just brimming with poison. Well, right now I could feel that poison seeping into me, like a horrible infection. No, this was not a place to linger. So I bent down. Then, just as I picked up my phone, the air began to move.

And there, forming in front of us, was Elsa Lenchester.

I was biting the inside of my mouth to stop myself screaming out with shock, as I really didn't want to give her that satisfaction. Dad was right beside me now, gripping my shoulder really tightly. I suppose we should have just legged it out of there, but we were so stunned we couldn't move.

Elsa Lenchester's dead venomous eyes fixed onto us. 'Don't look directly at her,' whispered Dad. But I didn't need telling about that.

'No one can ever stop us,' she screeched. 'We shall return – in triumph. Never doubt that, half-vampires!'

Then there was another rush of air. And suddenly, horrifyingly, a bolt of black lighting actually forked right across the room. And then she was gone.

I started to say something, but Dad shook his head at me and without another word we tore out of that cottage and into a world of rain. It was raining so hard I could hardly make out the car at first. Or maybe I was just too shocked by what I'd seen. Neither Dad nor I said one single word about it until we'd driven right away from there.

'Elsa Lenchester, what a show-off,' I said at last. 'But hey, I thought vampires couldn't return once they'd been humiliated.'

'They can't, normally,' said Dad, 'but a few have the power . . .' He hesitated.

'Yeah,' I prompted.

'To return in some form – very briefly.'

'The last time I saw her she was frothing and foaming at the mouth.'

'The shock was so violent she temporarily lost her poise,' said Dad, 'and the animal side of her nature took over. Full vampires are actually closer to animals than humans, and in moments of extreme anger or stress that breaks through. But she knew we'd return for your phone and wanted to deliver one final message to try and restore her battered pride. She won't go back there again.'

'But what about all her stuff?'

'Oh, she'll get another vampire to sort that out for her. The humiliation would be too keen for her to do that herself. She has been defeated, which is the cheering note in all this. But I'm very, very sorry I took you back there.'

'Hey, Dad, you weren't to know.'

'No, but I should have guessed. She was a vampire with really extraordinary powers. That's how she was briefly able to conjure up that lightning. She really wanted to shake us up one last time.'

'Well, she did that all right,' I said.

CHAPTER THIRTY

Saturday 17 November

8.00 p.m.

I'd just finished my tea when Mum and Dad sat down beside me with ultra-serious looks on their faces. Yeah, a big lecture was whizzing right at me. Actually I was surprised I hadn't had it sooner.

'On Wednesday, Marcus,' said Dad, 'I got such a terrible shock when Gracie rang me to say you'd got involved with vampires.'

'Er, just the one vampire actually, Dad,' I said.

'I didn't even tell your mother then,' said Dad. 'I was worried what hearing such terrible news over the phone might do to her, because I couldn't stop shaking when I heard.' He stopped and looked down. Mum squeezed his hand. 'No, I'm all right,' he croaked. 'And I've got a lot more to say, but it boils down to this really, Marcus. On Wednesday afternoon you gave me the worst time of my whole life. Nothing has ever been as bad as receiving that phone call.'

Wow! Dad really was laying it on now. Going right over the top. And I was about to say so until I suddenly remembered his face on that Wednesday afternoon when he was getting out of the car to rescue me. He'd looked so terrible; his face all white and stiff. And even now he looked an unhealthy hundred and five. And Mum only about a week younger.

I've done this to them, I thought. I've turned them into these two wrecks. And I really didn't know what to say to them. So instead I looked down and started counting my shoes. But I knew I had to say something so finally I said, 'I'm really, really sorry for causing you all that worry, and thanks for coming to rescue me, and I'll never forget what you did. I also want you both to know from now on I shall take up a much safer hobby – like swimming with sharks.'

'And do you promise us,' asked Dad, 'not to have anything to do with vampires again?'

'I do! Hey, now I feel as if I've just got married!' I grinned.

But Dad's face stayed tense. 'We've one other very important matter to sort out – Tallulah.'

A deep sense of unease rose in me. 'How do you mean, *sort out*?'

'What I mean is,' said Dad, 'we know the main reason you got involved with vampires is because of Tallulah. You and she are what I'd call best buddies.'

I swallowed down a smile at this description of Tallulah and me.

'By the way, she's not' – Dad gave a little embarrassed cough – 'your girlfriend, is she?'

'I don't think Tallulah could think of anything more insulting than to be called than that.' I grinned.

Dad shot Mum a look as if to say 'Told you so', and then went on, 'But she's your buddy who's . . .'

'Going through a very silly phase at the

moment about vampires,' said Mum. 'We did wonder if we should try and clear her mind of what she saw at the vampire's cottage.'

'No, you can't do that!' I shouted.

'It's all right. Calm down, please. We never need to raise our voices. We're having a calm discussion about this,' said Dad.

'OK, but you're not messing about hypnotizing her any more,' I said. 'She's had enough of that.'

'And we agree with you,' said Dad, 'especially as it might not be good for her so soon after she was put in that trance. And half-vampires *never* do anything harmful to humans.'

'So,' interrupted Mum, 'we have an alternative plan. It's very simple, actually. You, Marcus, must have nothing more to do with Tallulah.'

I hadn't been expecting this at all. I was stunned into silence.

'Now, we realize you may have to pass the time of day with her at school,' said Dad. 'But there can't be any more meetings. In fact, no contact at all out of school.'

I gaped at him. 'And just how long am I forbidden to talk to her?'

'Until she is over this silly obsession with vampires,' said Mum.

Well, I seriously doubted Tallulah would ever be over her fascination with vampires. So that would mean I'd never hang out with her again.

'It is dangerous for Tallulah to pursue vampires,' continued Mum, 'but far worse for us. For a vampire can spot our secret identity in a flash – and would have no hesitation in exposing us to humans either.'

I knew that was true. Hadn't Elsa instantly sussed out who I was and planned to make mischief by telling Tallulah as well?

'We realize we're asking a lot of you,' said Dad, 'but the truth is, we move in a different world to humans.'

'That's right,' I said bitterly. 'And ours involves hiding and pretending all the time, doesn't it?'

'I don't think,' said Dad, 'you'll find a human who doesn't also spend a great deal of his time hiding his true feelings and pretending to be happy when he's not. The only difference between us is that with us the stakes are so much higher. To protect our lives and our freedom, we have to pretend very well and can never afford to make even one single mistake. It also means, at times, making a very difficult sacrifice – like giving up, for the time being, a special chum.'

A special chum. He made Tallulah sound like a pet dog.

'I don't believe,' added Mum, 'you've got any choice. Not when you really think about it.'

I glared at her. What was making me so boilingly angry was that for once they were right. Tallulah will definitely be off pursuing more vampires, and if I carry on seeing her I'll be dragged along too.

And deep in my bones I knew I couldn't afford to do that. I'd had a lucky escape with Elsa. But next time . . . no, there mustn't be another time. I had to stop now. There was no alternative.

'So, please will you make us this promise not to see Tallulah out of school?' Dad's voice was soft, almost pleading. 'We won't follow you or check on you. We'll take your word. But we do want that promise.'

There was a beat of silence, then in a voice even quieter than Dad's, I whispered. 'Yeah, OK, I promise.'

Sunday 18 November

12.35 a.m.

Just back from a late-night flit. Managed twenty-seven minutes in the air tonight. A new record.

Afterwards Dad said, 'Soon, now, Fate's uncanny hand will be resting on you.'

'Say that again in English,' I said.

'I'm referring, of course,' said Dad, 'to your special power. You must be very excited about that.' And I was, from time to time.

'So when exactly is that checking in?' I asked.

'Soon,' said Mum eagerly, 'I think.'

'We don't know exactly,' said Dad, 'so try and be a little more patient. But what a chance awaits you. When I was your age I too had my first blood fever very early. And I was eagerly expecting a second one, as I so wanted to have a special power of my own.

But in fact I didn't get my second blood fever attack for another two months.'

'So, no special power?'

'No.' Dad sighed. 'It was not to be, and I ended up as just a very ordinary half-vampire.' He looked gutted about that even now.

1.20 p.m.

Just been imagining me taking on all the local bullies in one go. It'd be great if my special power makes me a brilliant fighter as I've always been total rubbish at that. Still, being able to send messages by telepathy was pretty cool too.

2.05 p.m.

Now I'm thinking of all the days and weeks stretching ahead – without Tallulah.

'There's always Gracie,' Mum has just said to me in the kitchen, and then added, 'and I know she's fond of you.'

And I like her and feel a really strong bond as well. In fact, I can't imagine my life without her. But Gracie isn't a consolation prize for Tallulah.

And I know the moment I tell Tallulah I don't want to trail after vampires any more – well, that's it, isn't it? She'll just walk away from me in total disgust and our friendship will be a thing of history. Knowing that turns me upside down.

But else can I do?

3.30 p.m.

I really dreaded telling Tallulah what I'd decided. And the moment has come much sooner than I'd expected.

You see, she's just turned up at my house.

CHAPTER THIRTY-ONE

Sunday 18 November

3.31 p.m.

When Tallulah turned up I was on my own.

My parents had left to meet someone who could advise them on how to bring out my special power. I thought it would just demonstrate itself one day, but apparently not. It has to be helped – or induced, as my parents put it.

Nothing about being a half-vampire is simple, is it?

So anyway, they said they wouldn't be long and I was to stay in today to give my body a chance to completely recover from the blood fever and my other recent exertions.

They'd only just left when the doorbell rang, and there was Tallulah.

She seemed out of breath too, as if she'd just run all the way here. And oddest of all – she gave me a small, tight smile. 'You look like Tallulah,' I said, 'but you can't possibly be her, because you sort of smiled at me. So you must be some sort of diabolical clone – so, tell me, what have you done to the real Tallulah?'

'Are you going to let me in – or what?' she asked quite good humouredly.

'Well, even though I have the gravest doubts as to who you really are, yeah, come in.'

I was so pleased to see her I almost danced to the kitchen. It was just so unexpected her turning up here. Surely I could enjoy this little moment before doing what I'd promised my parents I'd do.

'Tea, coffee, hot chocolate – or all three?' I asked.

'Surprise me.' She sat down at the kitchen table then and announced, 'Oh, by the way, I had an amazing time on Wednesday.' She said it just as if we'd been out on a date or something.

'So tell me,' I said, 'which part did you like best? Was it when that mad cat attacked you, or maybe it was the moment you were put into a trance . . . ?'

'I loved every second of it,' she said. 'Best day of my life.'

I was shocked by her enthusiasm – and yet I wasn't.

'You're not joking, are you?'

'Of course not, and by the way you weren't the total jerk I'd expected, either.'

Wow! A compliment from Tallulah – well, sort of.

'And the way you carried me out of that cottage on Wednesday,' she went on. 'That took nerve.'

'Not to mention strong muscles,' I quipped. 'You're quite a weight, you know.'

'Now, don't spoil it by making jokes – why have you got to be funny about everything?'

'I don't know, I just like laughing, I guess, and also I get nervous – especially when you're around.'

She didn't know how to respond to that. And we were both silent for a moment.

I slapped down a mug. 'This is called

coffee supreme, because it's actually tea . . .'

'You're doing it again,' she muttered.

'What!' I asked.

'Trying to be funny.'

'Sorry. OK, how's your flu?'

She didn't answer.

'But that was a serious question.'

She then said slowly, 'The thing is, Marcus, I didn't really have the flu.'

'Intriguing. So what did you have?' I asked.

'This is something I wouldn't want anyone else to know. All right?'

'Sure,' I said.

She lowered her eyes and, staring at the table, said in a low, flat voice, 'I went abroad with my family some time ago and while I was there, one person caught a rare bug. Not my obnoxious brother, not my truly awful sister. No, me.'

'So what was the bug you caught?'

'Some rare virus with a funny name which I can't even pronounce,' she said. 'And I was ill for ages and ages. And they kept doing all these tests and trying out masses of antibiotics on me. I was stuck in the house for weeks too, and with just my parents. I tell you, I nearly went insane.'

'I can imagine,' I said.

'But then I thought I was over it. And that's what my parents wanted me to think. One night, though, I heard them whispering downstairs, and they said how this bug had attacked my auto-immune system – I think that's right – and although I was in remission, it would keep coming back for years, and could . . . well, get much worse. But they weren't going to tell me any of this.'

'Only you know it now anyway.'

'Yeah, although my parents haven't a clue that I do know, and I pretend to believe them when they say it's just another nasty bout of flu. Recently my doctor and an important specialist turned up at our house. Mum said it was just as an extra precaution to check the flu wasn't getting any worse. That was the day, by the way, I was supposed to be trailing Giles Wallace with you. That was the real reason I couldn't come with you. Anyway, I've kept up the pretence of believing my parents.'

'But why?' I asked.

'I don't know,' she began.

'You just like fooling them, don't you?'

She half smiled. 'I suppose I do. But I did want to tell someone one day . . . and now I have. And amazingly it's you.' She looked at me expectantly.

But I just nodded. For what she'd said had gone so deep inside me that I couldn't speak at first.

'You're very quiet,' she said, half looking up at last.

'No, well, it's just . . . terrible to hear this.'

'Now you've really cheered me up.'

'Sorry, but you know what I mean,' I said.

'Well, I've had better news,' she said mockingly.

'And is there no cure?'

'None at all.' And she said this so lightly, while I felt all tight and empty inside.

'Still, I don't care,' she said. 'Well, I do, but I can't do anything about it, can I?'

I felt so sorry for Tallulah I wanted to get up and give her a big hug. But I had a feeling she wouldn't appreciate that at all.

'Will you stop looking so gloomy?' she cried. 'It doesn't suit you.'

'Sorry, but I just wish I could do something.'

'Well, you can't,' snapped Tallulah. 'And I *hate* people feeling sorry for me.' Her voice softened. 'There's good news too.'

'So what's that then?'

'When I was ill I was stuck in bed for weeks. And I really thought: I'm going to explode with boredom. But then I found these books on vampires. And from that moment I wasn't miserable or fed up any more. I just loved them. For vampires had such a bad attitude and were like angry all the time.'

'A lot like you then really,' I said.

And Tallulah beamed and took that as a great compliment. 'Yes, yes, exactly. And I just knew they couldn't only exist in stories. There had to be some bit of truth as well, and I was right. They are real. Only now, having seen one, up close—'

'You're not so keen,' I interrupted.

'They really are evil, aren't they?' she said.

'There's no argument about that,' I said, looking at Tallulah hopefully. 'So it's shattered your illusions about them?'

'Yes, it has,' she agreed. 'That's why I've just enlisted as a vampire hunter.'

I gaped at her. 'You've what?'

She looked up. 'I've had a couple of conversations with Giles. I've only just left him actually. I know you think he's a bit strange.'

'A bit!' I exclaimed.

'And yes, he does try too hard to be friendly, which can make him seem creepy. But he's really just very shy and a brilliant vampire hunter. He actually trailed the vampire here and was keeping watch in Brent Woods.'

I remembered how I'd spotted him there that night and just assumed he was the vampire.

'I know he'd have tracked Elsa down too if she hadn't used us to sabotage him. Anyway, he's staying on here. Being a tutor is just his cover, you see. Really he's working on the most important investigation of his life, as he believes we're right in the epicentre of further action by dangerous vampires – vampires like Elsa Lenchester. More are going to come here very soon. They've got to be found and stopped and he's recruited me to help do just that. What do you think?'

It was pretty obvious what Tallulah thought of it. She was all lit up and glowing.

Seeing me hesitate, she added, 'And don't worry about my health or anything deadly dull like that. After an attack I have a period of remission, sometimes quite a long one.' Her voice rose. 'And don't you see, Marcus, this is my chance to show I'm not just some poor sickly little girl who everyone should feel sorry for.'

'No one would ever think of you like that,' I said.

'But if they knew the truth, they would,' she said. 'So this is my opportunity to do something totally brilliant – and what could be better than saving the world from vampire monsters?' Before I could reply she shouted her own answer: 'Nothing, that's what! And you can be in on it too.'

'Me!'

'Yes, as I've asked Giles to recruit you as well. I told him all about what you did that day at Elsa Lenchester's cottage. And well, he wants to chat with you about our mission right now.'

'Our mission?'

That's what Tallulah was calling it already. I couldn't put it off any longer. Time to spout the words I'd promised my parents I'd utter. The ones I knew I *had* to say.

But then Tallulah cut in, 'I know you can't believe I want you to be in on this too, but I really do. Actually, I think we're a good combo.' And then she smiled at me again. Twice in one afternoon. This was a moment for the record books and no mistake.

But I couldn't hold back any longer. It wasn't fair to Tallulah. I gave a little cough. My throat felt so dry and my heart was thumping in my ears. 'The thing is, Tallulah, I'm pulling out of hunting vampires,' I said in a voice which didn't seem like mine at all. 'I just don't want to do it any more. Sorry.' The words had to be dragged out of my throat and now they all just hung there, in front of Tallulah and me.

For a moment she looked really shocked and hurt. But then she turned away from me and said in a muffled voice: 'Oh, that's a surprise.'

'I guess I just can't take the excitement any more,' I said feebly.

'OK then,' said Tallulah, really quietly and flatly. 'Anyway, I've got to go.'

'Are you going back to Giles?'

'Yeah, yeah . . . and I'll tell him what you said. It's fine.' Then she practically ran to the door, opened it and muttered, 'Bye then.'

'Look after yourself,' I called after her. But I don't think she even heard me, she'd sped away so quickly.

That was terrible, even worse than I'd expected, because Tallulah had really opened up and told me stuff she hadn't told anyone else.

And she'd said we were a 'good combo'. The very friendliest thing she'd ever said to me – or anyone else, I bet. And after all that, what do I do? Just kick her in the teeth. No wonder all the air seemed to have gone out of my body.

But I'm a half-vampire. I live in a different world to humans, so I *had* to say no. Hadn't I promised my parents exactly that? Now they would be proud of me.

But I couldn't ever speak to Tallulah again. Not properly. Something tightened in my throat.

I HAD NO CHOICE – or did I?

Suddenly I jumped to my feet. I was about

to do the maddest, stupidest, craziest thing of my whole life. But I couldn't let Tallulah down, not after what she'd told me today.

I just couldn't do that to her.

That's why I tore out of my house.

She was right at the top of my road. 'Tallulah!' I yelled.

She slowly turned round.

'Wait for me!' I shouted, and raced after her.

THE VAMPIRE BLOG

On his thirteenth birthday, Marcus Howlett
is faced with a bombshell. His parents are
half-vampires. And, although he hates the
thought of it, he is about to become one too.

But, as he secretly blogs about his
new fangs, cravings for blood and trying to
hide his secret from his vampire-crazy friend
Tallulah, Marcus is unaware that
his life is in serious danger . . .

And coming in 2012 –
the final story in the trilogy:

THE VAMPIRE FIGHTERS